Jason

by

Ana Balen

Self – Published by: Ana Balen
Edited by: Sean Hurdle
Cover design by: Veronique Poirier
Formatted by: Sean Hurdle
Zagreb, 2020

Chapter One

Jason

"Fuck," I hissed through clenched teeth, barely able to squash down the urge to roar in agony.

Even before my body hit the soft grass of the field, an excuciating pain radiated up my leg right to my stomach, threatening to bring back the salmon and veggies I had for lunch.

It was bad.

Really bad.

Possibly career-ending bad.

"Do. Not. Move," I looked up at the coach hovering over me, everything was hazy.

No shit, Sherlock.

I didn't say the words. I knew if I let them slip out, the club would slap me with a fine that would have even the toughest of men weeping like a schoolgirl after some punk kid pulled on her pigtails. What was worse, I would end up benched for the rest of the season. And that simply was not acceptable.

One thing that was absolutely forbidden as a Denver Thunders player was to mouth off to our coach. The coach wasn't the only man who had his hand firmly squeezed around all our balls. We had to do every single thing he said, and he was considered our God. He was that good.

And he deserved respect. Not only because he had our careers in his hands, but he also had the power to take it all away just by putting you on the bench. He also knew what he was doing. The man was the proud owner of eight fucking Super Bowl rings, and was supposed to help me get my first one.

First of many.

I was determined to give my all to bring glory to my team and maybe retire as the record-holding Quarterback in the history of Super Bowl rings. So yeah, fuck yeah, I squashed the words down my throat and bit my tongue for good measure.

"Get him off the field. We need to find out how big this fuck-up is."

I knew it was big. How big, was still yet to be determined. I couldn't grasp the fact of how the hell my foot stayed in place as my entire body turned to the right. Dylan pushed my shoulder down, preventing me from rolling over onto my side and trying to curl up into a protective ball. My leg was twisted in a way I couldn't comprehend. I was always careful running drills during practice, always on alert not to get into this kind of situation.

"The rest of you, start over, and I want to see real players and not little fucking girls jumping rope. This is not preschool, ladies," the coach roared, and unfortunately for me, blew his whistle just as he bent back down to hover over me...and that meant, right into my fucking ear.

Fucking perfect.

~~*

"What's the verdict, Doc?" I sighed the moment the door opened and a grim-faced man entered the room.

I had a feeling I wouldn't like the answer since the doctor's face stayed grim. I was ready to get out of this hospital room and head home.

After the assistant coach sprayed my ankle with something that made my joint and calf almost freeze over, the coach called an ambulance. Not even fifteen minutes later, I was transported to the hospital that took care of all the Denver Thunders players. When the doors of the ambulance opened, I could see the doctors running toward it, obviously, they stood there waiting for us at the entrance bay. They put me on this bed after an MRI, and the doctors right along with my coach went to pour over my scans, leaving me here alone for almost two hours. Alone, wondering what will happen, and not knowing if I would ever get the chance to go back to what I was meant to do.

Play football.

The only thing that made it better was the fact that the pain has subsided, but the swelling started to make my skin feel like it was going to split open at any second.

"You were lucky, Mr. Harris. The damage could be a lot worse; it's practically a miracle that all your ligaments and tendons weren't torn, I suspect it's only thanks to your excessive training and following our recommendations of eating right, taking all your vitamins, and not indulging in, let's say…unprofessional behavior, that this didn't become much worse," the doc started off by lecturing me.

I didn't need a lecture. I knew I was one slip from a fuck-up, so when doctors and trainers talked, I listened. I needed to know how extensive the damage was. And when I could go back to playing.

"Just say it," I demanded. I wanted to get out of there. There were reporters waiting for me to come out of the locker room, and I knew they were following the ambulance. I didn't have the patience to deal with them.

"Five weeks wearing the boot and at least six weeks of physical therapy," the doctor rattled off like it was nothing.

Fuck.

It was August.

With almost three months of recovery, it would mean I was out for almost the entire season. That is if the Denver Thunders made it to playoffs.

"Is there any way to get my man here back on the field sooner?" Curt, my manager asked.

Not even half an hour after I called him, he came barreling into the room, shouting at the nurses to get out of his way. I didn't want to, but he was the only person besides my teammates who could give me a ride home. I would be touched by his display of concern if the man wasn't all about the money I provided him. As he approached the bed, barely sparing me a glance, his beady eyes swept my body on their downward trajectory, and then fixated on my leg. There they stayed for the last fifteen minutes before the doctor came in.

"Ah, we could try with some cortisone shots, but I don't recommend that. Especially while playing."

"And why's that?" I asked, feeling my heart start beating faster, almost as if seeing the light at the end of the tunnel after all.

"Because you'll feel like you have full mobility and probably ignore our recommendations, which could end in a severe injury," the doctor simply shrugged his shoulders, familiar with the players' reactions and their lack of following doctors' recommendations.

"What if I promise to listen and follow your rules? I asked, since I couldn't let the opportunity for an earlier comeback slip through my fingers.

"Then I would have you come in every three days starting next week to have your shots, and we'll continue doing them through your physical therapy and slowly wind them down, both in frequency and the dosage," the doctor looked at me, not even blinking throughout his speech, daring me, assessing my reaction. "If you follow our every word, you should be back in the game two weeks earlier."

"Only two weeks?" the asshole standing next to my bed exploded. "He needs to be back in three weeks, ready to start the season."

"Done," I said, not looking away from the doctor.

I wanted, needed him to know I was dead serious. I also didn't want to give my manager the chance to do anything stupid, like suggesting to go find a different doctor, who would no doubt make things worse.
Not wanting to be shoved in a corner like a disobedient child, Curt growled, "We're going to need the best physical therapist there is."

The doctor looked to Curt, smiled a little, and after shaking his head, muttered, "Of course."

~~*

"I should come to Denver. You need someone to take care of you," my mother said into my ear, not really hiding the fact that she was crying.

"Mom, you don't need to do that. I'll be fine," I murmured in a soft tone, trying to get her to stop overreacting and keep her from doing something foolish.

Please God, stop her from getting some wild idea like jumping on a plane in the middle of the night to come here to fuss over me. Once she has it in her head, there's no way for anyone to stop her...not even Dad.

I loved my parents, especially my mom. God knows I did. But with the constant calls from her just to check how I was doing, or to hear my voice, or to tell me the latest thing my dad did, was driving me out of my mind. The last thing I needed was for her to come here and turn my place upside down, as it wouldn't meet her standards of what my home should look like. Every time she came to Denver for a visit, the moment she stepped over the threshold of my home, she would start to decorate it. I lost count of how many frou-frou bowls and toss pillows or the like I stuffed in the cubby that was my basement. She always complained it looked too manly and that it needed a woman's touch. It was only the fact that she did it all out of love for me and that I secretly enjoyed it, granted, not to that extent, that prevented me from being a total dick and demanding for her to stop. Also, I loved my mom and was confident enough in my manhood to admit I was indeed a mama's boy. To my mother's utter despair, I had no plans of finding the *right girl* and settling down.

Not right now.

Not when I finally had all I worked hard for most of my life for, minus the current situation. Though, I was confident it was just another bump in the road.

I'd make damn sure it was, and I wasn't going to fuck it all up by finding some god-awful woman whose entire life dream was to find an athlete and live her life spending his money and cutting his balls off, like most of my teammates did. Because many of my teammates ended up with such women, during away games, they ventured around the town to seek out an easy lay, just to feel something other than the frustration their wives constant nagging brought on. I did find a woman every now and then, but I was upfront. A no strings attached fuck that wouldn't lead to the altar.

"Are you sure?" my mom asked through another sniff, no doubt trying to get me to cave.

"Yes," I said firmly, so there wouldn't be any doubt.

"Jason…" she tried to say, probably get me to see her side on a long-suffering sigh, but I couldn't hear her words.

The sight that greeted me as I exited my bedroom made me stop listening and get a quick hold on the rage that started to boil. I kept my eyes fixed on the carpet until I calmed down just a little. Otherwise, I would strangle Curt, who was casually leaning against the kitchen counter.

Every available surface in the room was covered in beer bottles, pizza boxes, and condom wrappers.

"Listen, Mom, I have to go," I cut her off from whatever she was saying.

"Oh, that's right! You're meeting with your physical therapist today."

"Yeah," I mumbled, turned and sent a death glare to the man who completely ignored my warning signs, but was inspecting my fruit that was on the counter near him with mild interest.

"Call me after and tell me what his recovery plans are for you," she demanded in her mom voice, the one you don't ignore.

"I will, Mom," I lied. There was no way in hell I was going through another conversation like this today.

After saying goodbye, I tossed the phone to my right onto the TV stand and limped my way over to the coffee table to start the cleaning process. I hated this plastic thing I had to constantly wear, the showers were a bitch. Granted, it didn't itch like it would if I had a cast and it did serve its purpose, not to mention, reduced the need to depend on crutches. Thankfully, after four weeks of wearing the damned thing, it was finally time to take it off. I couldn't fucking wait.

"Had a good time last night?" I asked the ass who just stood there and didn't move a muscle to help me.

I didn't look up from picking up the garbage that was all over the place. I was scared I would lose my fucking mind if I saw the smirk on Curts face one more time. How the fuck had they managed to make such a mess?

When Dylan, Matthew, Logan, and Jimmy showed up at my door, each holding a six-pack, I knew I was in for a long haul last night. When Curt came with girls trailing into my living room, I'd had enough. I told them it was time to wrap things up and go find some other place to continue with the party. I was tired, and in pain. As I closed the door of my bedroom, I was aware they'd ignored me, but I wasn't willing to do anything about it. I just had one thing on my mind, to lie down, because the shot of cortisone was wearing off, and my ankle was throbbing. They all frequently made fun of me for living in a house and not in some mansion, but they sure liked to spend time here and bring their latest hook-ups. It was a tactic that worked well for them since none of the girls found out where they lived, and they had no way of finding out. It was the reason I had a lock on my bedroom door. It was also the reason I, at least twice a week, had to call the cops to escort women away who were camping outside, waiting for the moment my teammates would show up.

This shit had to stop.

I was getting tired of the boys hanging at my house almost every night. After living in Denver for almost a year, I knew it was high time to go out and meet some new people. The only problem with that, all I did was play football or go to practice. And every now and then, the guys were fun to hang with. I loved my place, usually. It wasn't too big and I could take care of it myself. I also knew what NFL stood for...Not For Long...so I had my money safely tucked away in a savings account for when the moment came I needed to retire, I would be able to do it comfortably and not freak out without a plan. I would have the luxury of taking my time of figuring out what I wanted to do with my life without the fear of not having an income hanging over my head, and the main reason why I still put up with Curt, the man was one

of the best in his business. I was aware that he was the one
who got me the deal with Thunders, not only my ability on
the field.

"Yep," Curt said, popping the P. "You should have stayed
with us and not gone to bed like a ten-year-old when the
clock struck ten-thirty."

"You know my schedule. You also know there's nothing
more important to me than to get back in the game. You
further know I don't want any partying in my home," I once
again reminded Curt.

My jaw was clenched so tight, my teeth hurt. It was
alarming how frequently Curt asked me to go out to the
clubs and find some easy girls for the night. One would
think, being my manager and all, he would be first in line to
get me to live a life of sacrifice required of a professional
athlete.

"Oh, relax, Jason." He waved me off like it was no big deal.
"We just had a few beers and a good time. It wasn't as if we
trashed the place."

It wasn't like they trashed the place?

I kept my mouth shut; I only looked around then back to my
manager and cocked a brow at him. At least the man had the
decency to swallow hard and turn around to help throw out
the trash from the mess they made last night. I was just
hauling the last of the trash bags away when there was a
knock at the door.

I could hear Curt open the door, then chuckle as he said in a
patronizing tone, "Sorry, sweetheart, whoever you're
looking for, he's not here."

Before he could close the door on the poor girl looking to find her athlete and promptly start planning the wedding, a throaty voice said, "Ummm… I'm looking for Jason Harris. The hospital gave me this address. I'm Rory Ryan, his physical therapist."

Standing in the kitchen, I could see the stunned look on Curt's face and a small hand reaching in, trying to shake the asshole's hand. Limping as fast as I could, I hurried to get to the door. I fully planned on slapping Curt on the back of his head to get him to stop gawking at whoever was standing in front of him and let my therapist in. My plan came to a halt when the sight that had Curt transfixed met my eyes. There, in the bright Denver sun, stood a tiny woman with honey-blonde hair that barely reached her shoulders. A pouty mouth that had the most perfect Cupid's bow I have ever seen, and big hazel eyes that kept shifting nervously between the two of us. Pulling back her arm, she shook her head and licked those perfect lips. I was dying to know if nectar would leak out if I bit them.

"I'm sorry for disturbing you. I probably have the wrong address."

Those words and her soft tone made something in my gut jolt as I reached out, grabbed her wrist and gave it my all to ignore the electrifying current that shot through my palm right to my dick. I would be surprised if she didn't catch the fact that I was intrigued by her. If I wasn't so angry, I would have realized she obviously didn't have the same reaction to me. Instead, she tried to dismiss me, not to mention dared to try and take away the most alluring sight I have ever seen, that being herself.

"No, no," her startled yes came to mine. "You're at the right place. I'm Jason Harris."

"Nice to meet you, Jason Harris. I'm the one who's going to torment you for the next six weeks."

Watching her mouth move as she said those words, I had no doubt what she said was absolutely true. I knew the smile she fixed on her beautiful face, the same one that made her eyes twinkle, was going to haunt my dreams.

Chapter Two

Rory

"Please," Jason gestured for me to take a seat at his couch. "Would you like something to drink?"

I could really go for some coffee, since the effect of the last one I had was starting to wear off, and thanks to my asshole brothers who kept me awake for most of the night, I really needed another. Still, I shook my head a little, declining. It was better for everyone if I got some on the way home, because if it wasn't done just the way I liked it, it wouldn't be pretty. For some reason, people tended to look at me funny, slowly backing away when I voiced that the coffee wasn't done correctly. If they offered me some, they should be able to follow the instructions. It isn't my fault that most of the population are certified idiots.

"No, thank you," I muttered, looking around the place.

It wasn't what I expected Jason house to be. Stepping inside, I was able to see everything as it was one huge, open space. On the left, there was a coat closet, and next to the door was a bench where you could sit and take off your shoes. When you turned right, the first thing you could see was a fire place that had grey tiles with black-ish veins in them, going all the way up to the ceiling. In front of the fire place was a couch that could easily seat four people, and in front of the couch was a glass coffee table with chrome legs. On the mantle of the fire place were some picture frames, but I didn't have a chance to look closely and see what pictures were important enough for Jason to have on display.

As I continued into his house, I could see another couch and two chairs arranged in front of a huge TV mounted on the wall. Beyond that was the rectangular dark wooden table with eight chairs. What made the dining room perfect were the French doors, from there you could see the backyard and the greenery of his lawn.

I turned right again, stopped and froze immediately. I saw the most perfect kitchen ever. It was big, it was masculine, and it had two freaking islands with barstools, three to be exact, positioned in front of them. The mix of grey and steel went perfectly together. Even the farmers sink fit in like it was invented just for this kitchen only. The entire house was a mix of grey, white, and black. The sharp angles of Jason's furniture didn't look intimidating, but sophisticated. Definitely a surprise.

I came out of my stupor and followed Jason as he stood near the first couch and asked me to sit. I took a seat on the surprisingly comfortable couch, but upon leaning back, I felt something poke me. Then, a rude voice got my attention, and I looked up.

"How in the hell do you think you'll be able to be Jason's therapist? Look at him, then look at you."

I did just that, looked at Jason, that is. The man was beyond handsome. Dark brown hair, with just the right number of blond strands in it, which just by looking at them I knew came from being out in the sun and not a bottle. It was a sad fact that nowadays, women had to go to battle for hair color, while for men it came naturally. His brown eyes reminded me of coffee grounds, but then again, that could be just me imagining it, thanks to the lack of caffeine in my blood. High cheekbones, thin lips that for some unexplainable reason look really soft, and a five o'clock shadow decorating his square jaw. Not to mention all the muscles, that even in his relaxed posture, looked flexed and powerful. The man was simply delicious. I could see the other man's point, and a few years ago, I would have suggested they find someone else to work with Jason, but after working so hard and becoming one of the best in my field.

Entering the prestigious league to be able to work with professional athletes, I wasn't going to cave. Especially when I saw the smirk Jason was wearing, probably thinking he could intimidate me and get me to leave.

"My eyes work just fine," I drawled, feigning disinterest and trying not to fidget as that mysterious thing kept poking me in my lower back. "I'm confident that if Mr. Harris will listen to my instructions, we'll be able to work together just fine."

"And would you be able to keep your hands to yourself and not try to get my client to fuck you, so you could get whatever the hell you women want?"

Wow, the man was hands-down the biggest jerk I ever had the displeasure of meeting.

"Oh, I'm quite positive that will be avoided," I said, feeling satisfaction when Jason's smirk was wiped clean off his face when he heard my words.

Sure, he was the most beautiful man I'd ever seen, and that moment when he touched my skin still had me discreetly clenching my thighs, trying to relieve the pressure building between my legs, but I'd be damned if I ever let him do anything even remotely suggestive. I knew his type. Not this handsome, but the athlete in him. They had women falling down on their knees, begging them to fuck them, wherever they went. And usually, they took the offer. I mean, who wouldn't? I also knew, from past experience, that they asked for it if you didn't offer. I don't know how many times I had to shut a player down and tell him there was no way in hell I would ever have sex with him, give him a blowjob, or let him *rock my world*, as they put it. Just because I was rubbing the man's thigh didn't mean I wanted to give him a hand-job, for Christ's sake. It was a massage, and they needed to learn it didn't come with a happy ending. I also knew that most of said players were shit in bed. People talk, and sure, there are some of my co-workers who do this just to get their player and all that comes with him.

"Let's move on." Jason cleared his throat, and after running his eyes up and down my frame, making every hair on my body stand at attention, he quirked a brow as I squirmed. "Let me see your recovery plan."

I couldn't take it anymore. I had to reach behind my back and move whatever it was that was now bruising my skin. Pulling out a red bra, I gave him a look, finally gaining the upper hand.

"There isn't one," I started to explain and had to put my hand up to stop both men from talking when they opened their mouths. "Tomorrow morning, I'll meet you at the hospital when your boot is taken off. Judging by your constant glaring at it, I'm guessing it was probably good they didn't give you the key."

"I could have gotten the key?" he asked in surprise, giving the brace another glare.

It irritated me how cute he looked while doing it. And I doubt he was even aware he was doing it, which of course made it even cuter.

"After, we'll go to the training center and do a light stretching of the joint. You don't want to start exercises at least for a few days, as the joint is stiff, and if we put too much strain on it before we loosen it up, it could do more damage than good." Finally, he was giving me a serious look, hanging on my every word, and not looking at me like I was a joke. "Then, we'll do some exercises, including walks and, after a few days, runs. And last, we'll add in weights. In between, you'll get the daily massage to loosen up your muscles, again so the joint will be loose. At first, you will have therapy, and down the road, we'll discuss when to have it two times a day." I had to admit, I was proud of myself for coming up with a semblance of a plan in under five seconds.

"When can he start training?" The question came from the jerk who stood behind my patient, but I gave my answer to Jason.

"The first assessment still stands. Granted, you did manage to shave off a week of wearing the boot. Unfortunately, I can't say how long it'll take for you to be fully functional and come back to playing without putting yourself into jeopardy of a repeated injury." I hated that I couldn't give him the news he wanted to hear, and when his face fell, I had to look away or I would get up, hug him and stroke his hair.

God, What the hell was going on with me?

The sound of a throat clearing lassoed my eyes back to Jason. He had a tentative smile on his face as he nodded his head and said, determination steeling his voice, "Let's do this."

~~*

"Hey, boo," I whispered to my black cat who waited for me to come home and graciously gave me the opportunity to scratch her behind her ears.

That is, until two seconds later, when she decided I had enough of the gift she was giving me and promptly turned her back, her tail sticking in the air like an antenna, and at a leisurely slow pace went to my kitchen, where she regally awaited me to do my sworn duty of feeding her. Usually, that would irritate me, the fact that she considered me her servant and not fulfilling my dream of her being my pet I could snuggle with, but today, it only served as a reminder I was home and could finally relax. It was a meeting from hell with Jason, where Curt, his manager, as I was informed by the man himself, demanded I first find Jason a suitable therapist. After I phoned the club and they assured him I was indeed the best, which I'll admit left me a little smug, he then proceeded to question my every word. I grabbed a cup of coffee and went to the clinic to pick up Jason's scans and medical history. Thankfully, I was able to avoid Niles, one of the male nurses who got it in his head that his sole purpose on this earth was to fuck me, and his attempts became creepier by the day, and got out without incident.

After putting my stuff away and looking dreadfully at the stack of papers and scans that awaited me to go through later, I went to the kitchen to do what was demanded of me by increasingly louder meows. I loved my place; it was everything I ever wanted…for now. I was determined not to go down the road my mom did and be financially dependent on some man. I knew if I worked hard and saved what I could, one day I would be able to fulfill my dream and own a house. My mom did her best, but after my dad got killed, working two jobs and taking care of four children became too much. Not that I blamed her. My brothers were the reason I got into physical therapy and always had a secret stash of bail money.

So, after five years of trying to take care of everything by herself, she caved and got married to Nate, the man she was seeing at the time. Normally, my brothers and I wouldn't have had an issue with her remarrying. Teresa Ryan was too beautiful of a woman to spend the rest of her life on her own, but our dearest step-dad was a complete and total jerk. He not only constantly reminded her that he was the one who kept a roof over our heads and food in our tummies, but he also went as far as to actually expect my mom to wait on him with dinner ready, demanding to be served, all while she still worked two jobs. Sometimes, and that was before my brothers went into their growth spurt, he would give her threatening looks until she cut his food.

So, five years ago, when I found her sitting on her bed with tears silently going down her face and longingly looking at a picture of my dad, I had enough. It took some convincing, but I made her see reason, opened her eyes to the fact that all her kids had grown up and lived on their own, and got her to divorce the asshole. I thought I could finally breathe once the divorce papers were signed, but I was wrong. Before the ink was dry, Teresa decided she could start living her life again and started playing the field. When my thoughts went down the dangerous road of my mom dating, I shook my head, threw my bag on the floor, and hung my coat. I didn't need the torture of dreading what kind of mess she would end up in now, and I also didn't want to call my brothers and ask if there were any new developments.

I loved my family, adored them, but they were exhausting sometimes.

The two-bedroom apartment was my sanctuary. Open floor plan with the kitchen right across from the door, a round table that seated six with a glass vase in the center of it that held four white calla lilies. On the left was a cream couch and chair in front of which stood a brown low coffee table, and farther on the wall hung the big TV. The best part of it all was the big arched windows next to the table that poured the natural light in every corner.

"Here you go, Miss," I murmured to my cat, stealing a few more scratches, which she ignored.

I turned and went down the short hallway that had doors on each side. On the right, it was my makeshift gym. I needed to gain and secure my strength to work all the kinks and aches out of the athletes' muscles, which were firmer than stone. At least it seemed that way. Opening the door on the left, I entered my bedroom, and not looking up, went straight to my bathroom to my most prized possession…my tub. Turning the hot water knob, I plug the drain and let the water fill the tub.

"Finally, heaven," I moaned into the empty bathroom, my voice echoing around the steam-filled room as I lowered myself into the hot water.

I knew that at least three hours of work waited for me in my living room. I had to go through Jason's medical history, but as I closed my eyes, his image started dancing behind my closed lids, and the ghost of his touch prickled across my skin, and I really couldn't care less.

Chapter Three

Rory

"When will you finally tell us who your new patient is?" Max asked me around a mouthful of burger.

I had every intention of having a quiet and relaxed night home, right after a good hour of soaking in my tub, because God knew I needed it after the day I had. But my oldest brother had other plans. Seeing him the moment I turned the corner as he leaned on the wall next to my bedroom door, holding a bag of takeout containing only one burger and French fries…selfish bastard…I knew my day from hell wasn't over.

First, I overslept and ran late for Jason's appointment. I stayed up way too late, studying his medical records and scans. Once his cast was removed, we went on to our first therapy session. Overall, I was actually impressed with the guy. He was in perfect shape, all his random drug tests came back negative, and there was no record in any gossip magazine articles that Google could find of him stumbling out of some nightclub drunk. I checked. I had my suspicions about him being one of those guys who partied all night only to come to practice hung over. It wasn't unheard of, especially in football. But the guy was squeaky clean.

The moment I stumbled into the exam room, still on my first cup of coffee, the questions started.

"Do you have a therapy plan?"

"How long do you think before I can start with practice?"

"What are we going to do today?"

"Don't you think, since I have dedicated my life to the sport, I should be able to go through the phases you said yesterday much faster than others?"

I just stood in the corner of the bright room, trying to hide from the sunlight pouring in through the windows, rubbing my temples and praying to God that I could stop my normal reaction when someone dared to speak to me before I finished with my first cup and not cry. The strong scent of alcohol and other hospital odors didn't help either. I had no other choice in the end but to give the man, who starred in my dreams last night doing all the naughty things to me known to man, the death glare and growl, "Shut up!"

His eyes closed dangerously to slits and he opened his mouth, but I got there before him, cutting him off in time. "No! What you need to understand is you're the one who needs *me*. You can't do this without me, and I hate to break it to you, but I'm your best shot at a full recovery." Okay, maybe I did let myself get a little smug on that last part. It was my full right after all, since I worked my butt off to be where I was. "You're going to do exactly what I tell you to do, to the very last letter. You're not going to bitch at me, whine, beg, or any other thing along those lines, especially before I've had my first cup of coffee." Which reminded me to take a sip, just to get a little more patience for the man. *"Now, be nice, shut up, and leave me alone. Don't open your pretty mouth and try to speak. I need total silence if I want to finish my coffee, so we can prevent me from wringing your neck."* The last I muttered to myself, but when I chanced a peek at his face, I was pretty sure he heard me. If the mix of stunned and smug look that was gracing his beautiful face was any indication.

After Jason sent one last grim look to the brace that the blushing and giggling nurse was holding, I picked up my bag and waited for him to hobble to me so we could get going. That was after she basically crawled all over him under the guise of checking if he was all right, through which Jason just sent her polite little smiles and darted his eyes all over the place. I pushed away the sudden urge to bitch-slap her and instructed Jason to follow me to the therapy area. I hadn't even taken one step out of the exam room when his words stopped me. "No, we have to go to my place."

"No, we don't," I said slowly, trying to remain calm when everything in me was screaming just to say fuck it and quit. We weren't working together even a whole day, and I was close to walking away. "We have everything we need right here at the hospital."

At my words, for some reason, a slight blush crept up his neck to his face. He looked down and rubbed the back of his neck with his hand, his flexing muscles a siren song for my eyes to track them.

"I'm sorry, but I can't come here every day. I don't know how, but the press and fans got word that I'm here, and at least twenty of them are waiting at the entrance for me to come out. There's no telling how many of them will be camping here as I come in each day, and I'm sure you want the hospital to function properly and take care of its patients."

I had to admit he was right. I almost got trampled when entering the place.

"Fine," I sighed, turned then walked out of the room leaving Jason with a stunned look on his face.

After a cortisone shot, arranging for me to be the one who will administer them in the future, a short detour to the children's ward, where he gave autographs and posed for pictures, and sneaking off to go to his place, another form of torture began. I didn't want to admit it, but I had a newfound respect for the man. Seeing the smiles on the kids' faces, not to mention how much fun Jason appeared to have, the anger for constantly questioning me I held toward him started to rapidly melt away, and he started to simply annoy me.

I could still feel my palms tingling from the touch of his skin. From the moment I started stretching his joint until the very last second of the leg massage, I had to clench my teeth and my thighs, because the prickly sensation shot from my palms right to my breasts, making them swell until it settled in my clit, which pulsed with my every heartbeat. Thankfully, Jason questioning my sanity and my will to kill him helped push the urge to bring his head down so I could kiss him and call him all the filthy, sexy names that exist away. He made me want him more and more with every second that passed.

"You're aware that we're not going to give up?" Max asked, bringing me to the present.

I looked at him sideways, assessing the truth in his statement. I loved him as I did all my brothers. I just wished they didn't frequently drive me to the point of committing homicide or spend so much money on bail. Considering how much time they spent in a holding cell, it was a miracle they could keep their jobs. Then again, all the guys from the station thought it was hilarious whenever I called them to get those brutes out of my way. A few years ago, they even gave me an envelope full of cash. It turned out to be bail I paid over the years. So, at least that mystery was solved. They didn't get officially arrested and processed; they were just holding them there, so I could get a few hours of peace.

"Yeah, I know," I sighed and decided, since he ambushed me in my own apartment, scaring the daylight out of me when he growled, demanding I tell him who it was, I had every right to eat his french fries.

"Hey!" He tried to get them back but pulled his hand back quickly when I retaliated. "Not fair, you know you're not allowed to use your knowledge or put pressure on our nerves to cause us pain. I'm going to tell Mom."

I rolled my eyes at him to let him know how much that pained me and continued speaking as if he hadn't said a word. "And you know I can't tell you who my patient is, as I never can, but you're still going to drive me crazy trying to find out who it is."

"It would be best for everyone if you just told us," he said in a condescending tone and shrugged his massive shoulders. "You know we won't give up."

"And you also know there's no way in hell you're going to find out," I replied, knowing it won't help.

"There's three of us and only one of you," he gave me a cocky wink before he took his next bite.

Finishing the last of his French fries, I swallowed, bunching up a napkin. "Just… please don't make me spend any more money on bail."

"It was your fault the last time!" he shouted in outrage. "What sane person calls the cops on their brothers?"

"The same one who thinks someone's breaking in at three in the morning, you jerk."

God, could it be so difficult to give me normal, loving, protective brothers instead of the three lunatics I got stuck with? Is that too much to ask?

"Finish your dinner and get out. I need to get some sleep."

Pushing away from the table, I took my bag and papers that were on the couch with me, so the big brute wouldn't get any ideas, and went to my room, leaving him sitting at the table. "And no more breaking in!" I yelled as I stashed the papers that would give Jason's identity away behind three boxes of tampons. If one thing scared the living hell out of them, it was lady products.

Looking behind me, I checked if the coast was clear and started to take my clothes off almost giddy for my bath.

"You do know mom has a new boyfriend, right?" Max asked, standing behind me and making me scream.

Oh, fucking hell.

Chapter Four

Jason

"Are you sure you're not trying to kill me?"

It was the fifth time I asked Rory that question in the span of the seven days we've worked together, and every time I asked, she glanced up at me with that look that screamed *you're a dumbass*. I battled a constant urge to either throttle her, or take her in my arms and kiss her before I proceeded to fuck the daylights out of her.

The restraint I had on my control was slipping today. It was because I had a full week of her tormenting me under the excuse that she was helping me heal. Her bending down to help me do the exercises, with her heart-shaped ass right in front of my face, making saliva pool in my mouth, was pure torture. I wanted to lick it or take a bite out of it so badly. Her rubbing her hands all over me under the guise that she was massaging my sore muscles that screamed in agony, all the while I just had to lie there and fight the hard-on she was giving him, was not helping either. It was all becoming just a tad too much.

I was just a man, for God's sake.

I didn't know how much of this I could take.

I didn't feel any better from all the pain enduring therapy. In fact, every night, my leg hurt like a bitch, making me limp even more than I did when I had the brace. Granted, my ankle wasn't stiff in the mornings like it used to be, and the limping wasn't bad during the day either. If I was honest with myself, I could see the progress and slowly the pressure subside each day. I was truly impressed with her knowledge of sports injuries, but I would be damned if I ever said that out loud. Also, her work ethic was something that I admired more and more. I couldn't even count how many phone calls I overheard during which she rattled all the medical phrases like she was reading a phone book or giving instructions on how to properly do the exercises.

I caved once and asked what all that was about. I was sure that she would simply shrug her shoulders and say it wasn't my business. But, she surprised me when she said that they were the calls from her previous patients, all while trying to hide a blush that crept up her neck to her cheeks. When I asked if they were famous athletes, she had a stubborn look her face and told me to shut the hell up and do as I was instructed. I took it as a yes. The most surprising thing was, she didn't brag or thow out the names of people I may have known just to impress me. She seemed genuinely shy about it, and that brought me to another problem. That afternoon, I began to admire her and as the days went by, I started to feel pride. She let her work speak for itself. And fuck me, but it was hot as hell.

"Ouch!" I yelped, giving Rory a murderous glare. Any other girl would jump up and try to make me feel better, fawning all over me, trying to take the pain away.

But not Rory.

No.

All she did was look up at me from where she was squatted down while she rotated my joint this way and that, and winked at me, giving me a little smirk. That was it. I was going to fire her. I had no other choice. Day in and day out she was slowly and painfully killing my career. Not to mention, making my dick weep in agony in the process.

It was a shame really. The fact that I absolutely had to do it. I liked having her around, bending every few minutes, granting me the full view of that heart-stopping ass, or just like now, squatting down and giving me the chance to peek down her shirt at her mouthwatering breasts.

Yeah, no woman, no matter how attractive she was or how many cold showers I had to take after she was gone was worth me losing my spot in the Denver Thunders. It irritated me to no end that she, did in fact, know what she was doing, and I wasn't about to fall for her career-killing plans. But, I would just find another therapist that was just as good; I didn't care how much it cost or where in the world the person lived.

On top of it all, I hated those few times that I overheard her phone conversations that weren't with her former patients and those soft *I love you too's* that she whispered before she hung up. At first, I was furious that she obviously had a man in her life, and that made me want to tear out the walls in my proximity with my bare hands. As soon as I convinced myself it was only because I wanted her to be focused only on me for the duration of our contract and nothing more, I found out it was either her mother or her brothers on the other end of the line. Well, my reaction to that little tibit was even more frustrating, since I wanted all those soft words for myself, and as soon as I got confirmation she was single, something in me sighed in relief.

So, fuck yeah, it was time for her to go and for me to finally start living as I should. Free of her, and focused only on coming back to the field.

"Listen, Rory," I started his practiced speech, only for my eyes to cross over and my head to fall back, lolling on my shoulders.

I had to use every ounce of my strength to trap the moan that wanted to come out of my mouth as she started massaging my leg. I could swear I heard her soft chuckle, but I couldn't be sure and I didn't give a damn as long as her little hands traveled upward. Almost as if she heard me, she did just that, pushing her apt fingers deep inside the muscle tissue and relaxing every single nerve I had in my body.

"Oh yeah, baby, just like that," I muttered.

"I take it you like it," she was now openly laughing at me.

Hearing her mirth, my head whipped up and I had to clear my throat before I could give her a stern look and talk. "Yeah, yeah. It feels okay."

Just a little bit higher, the thought invaded my mind, *just a little bit to the right.*

No matter how hard I tried, I couldn't look away from her hands and stop, willing for her to move them so they would cover my dick that was, to my horror, getting harder by the second. As she made her way to the middle of my thigh, I brushed her hands away abruptly and reached for the towel that was next to me on her portable table she demanded that I have, so I could cover up.

"Don't worry about it," she said casually like it wasn't a big deal. Even though I damn well knew it was, my dick was a big deal. Not looking away for a second from my legs, she switched to my right leg as if nothing happened and started talking. "It's the body's normal reaction to this." She looked up at me and, swallowing hard, she finished on a whisper, "It's because of the increased blood flow."

Once, just once, I would've liked to see I wasn't the only one who was affected.

"I hate you. You know that, right?" I could feel the muscle jumping in my cheek and was actually afraid I would grind my teeth to dust.

"You do now, but you're going to love me in the end."

The infuriating woman winked at me again and went right back to work, leaving me with nothing to say. I was too afraid she was right.

~~*

"Fuck," I hissed as the first spray of freezing water landed on my aching cock.

Rory left two hours ago, and no matter what I did, I could not get the fucker to play nice and accept that it wouldn't get what it wanted. I knew I could just take myself in my hand and give in to fantasies of Rory riding my dick, her B-cup tits jumping up and down in front of my face, but that play was dangerous. Without a shred of doubt, I knew that if I gave in and went down that road, it was only a matter of days that I'd have to have her. Pushing my palms against the black tiles of the shower, I took a step back and away from the cold spray so my dick wouldn't freeze and fall off. Leaving my palms firmly on the ceramic, I leaned forward, hoping the cold blast on my head would help me cool down. Maybe if my brain got shot with cold water enough, I would be able to get a full night's sleep without the little pain in my ass coming to visit my dreams. Making this need that coursed through me pulse with every heartbeat, growing stronger and bringing me to the brink of insanity.

Fuck, but just thinking about those dreams, I couldn't help but wonder how responsive she would be. How her perfect-sized tits would feel in my palms. They weren't too big or too small. No, Rory's were just the size I liked, and I knew I could take her whole tit in my mouth. Would her nipples be small or big, light or dark pink? How would they taste in my mouth as I bit on the soft flesh lightly, then suckled them enough to relieve the pain? Would her pussy weep for me to take her? How tight would she be? Would she scream my name when she came? Would she scratch my back with those short nails of hers as I plunged into her? Damnit, but just thinking of it made my saliva pour into my mouth and my vision became blurry.

"Fuck," I hissed when I realized that in my musings about the intolerable woman, my hand started slowly going up and down my dick.

I should've stopped right then. I should've taken an ice bath and chased away all the images of Rory swimming in my head. But fuck me, just the thought of her short, strong legs wrapped around my waist made my cock weep with precum.

"Fucking hell," I growled as I watched my hand gliding up and down faster, squeezing the head of my dick.

Images of Rory moaning in my ear, her body squirming under me, and screaming my name after I gave her the best orgasm of her life, had me gasping for air as my balls drew up, the pain in my now ever harder dick becoming almost unbearable.

"Rory," I hissed, and watched as shot after hot shot flew from my stubborn dick and landed on my tiles, the stark contrast of my white cum and the black tiles mocking me.

The last image that shot through my head was me decorating Rory's stomach in my cum, all while she was the one giving me a handjob.

Christ, did I just fantasize about a hand job?

I did

Now I knew deep inside I was well and truly fucked.

"Don't do it, you jackass," I said to myself as I stepped out of the shower and reached for the towel to dry off before I went to do what just became an absolute no moments ago.

As I shut off the light in the bathroom, going into my bedroom and pulling up jeans, I shook my head and almost barked, "Do not fucking do it."

The whole time, as I went out of my house, right to my car, and before I came to her door, I was giving myself every chance to turn around and try to forget what happened in my bathroom, but I knew there was no coming back from it. I wanted her as much as I wanted to go back to playing football. I needed her as much as I needed the rush of a touchdown from one of my passes. My heart beat faster, giving me life, giving me purpose when I was near her just as much as the roar from the crowded stadium did.

No, there was no going back.

Because Rory Ryan was mine.

It's just a matter of convincing her, I thought, still shaking my head at my own stupidity of ever thinking the opposite when the blood in my body turned cold.

"Stop it, you fucking bastards!" the high-pitched sound of my woman screaming in terror behind the door.

Chapter Five

Rory

"Stop it, you fucking bastards!" I shrieked, foolishly thinking it was going to stop the idiots who were tearing my beautiful apartment apart, trying to find out Jason's identity.

I should have known better. Any other time, if I even raised my voice, they would come and one of them would pat my body down, looking for injuries, while the others would be trying to find the threat so they could demolish it.

But not now.

No.

After a week full of break-ins, thankfully during the day, ambushes at the least expected places, whining, pleading, begging, and attempted bribing, they had enough. And the three dickheads came together and figured that the best course of action was if all three came and ruined my sanctuary. I was bending down to Carter, who I thought was the good brother and had my back in this insane obsession of theirs, and who was currently knocking on my hardwood floor after he flipped my white couch so he could get under it. He was muttering *there has to be one*. What, I didn't know?

I whispered, "I'm calling Mom if you don't stop," when suddenly there was a loud banging on my door, shaking it on its hinges.

Great, who had they called for reinforcements?

I didn't get to take one step to my poor door, when Chace ripped it open, turned around to look at me, put his hand to his chest, and gasped, "You bitch!" before the cacophony of shouts.

"I knew it!"

"Dear God, we hit the motherload!"

And mayhem ensued.

~~*

"I'm disowning you. You no longer exist," Max sniffed when I came into his line of vision.

"Is that the way you greet your savior?" I asked, raising my brow to the giant who was my big brother.

"Savior?" he snorted and looked at me through the bars. "You're the one who put us here."

"No, the nice police officers who came are the ones who put you here."

"And who called them?" Chace asked in outrage.

Dear God, save me!

I couldn't understand how three adult males in their thirties could possibly behave like that. It was no wonder neither of them had girlfriends. Despite their various shades of blond hair, astonishing green eyes, and sculpted bodies, they were all still single. Yes, they were my brothers, but even I had to admit they were good-looking.

I chanced a glance at Jason, who was quietly sitting on the bench opposite them, wearing a stunned look on his face.

He didn't say a single word to me. Not before the cops came, or after. Not even now, while those three were sending me death glares.

"I'm sorry you ended up in here. That's not what I wanted," I whispered to him, scared of his reaction and crossing my fingers he wasn't going to fire me.

"What about our apology?" Max demanded.

"What apology?" I asked, still looking at Jason, who remained silent still not looking away from three idiots sitting opposite him.

"We're here because of you, too!" he yelled. "How could you call the cops on your own flesh and blood?"

"Because you were trying to tie me up and kidnap Jason!" I yelled right back, noticing the female police officer sighing as she came to stand by me and look at Jason.

"Bullshit," Carter said, pulling my attention from the woman and stopping me from spending the night in a cell. "We were just trying to take the man out, show him a good time." He shrugged. "You know, wine and dine."

"And what about tying me up?" I asked at the same time Jason finally spoke, his tone incredulous.

"You wanted to take me out on a date?"

"Yes!" all three of them said in unison.

Jason started to turn his head my way but decided not to when Max said, sniffing, "You should consider yourself lucky. After all, we are a catch."

"I'm sorry, but who are you?" He shook his head in confusion, leaving the subject of a date with three men alone.

All of them gave him charming smiles as Chace said, "We're your future brothers-in-law."

~~*

"Sit down," I said, not looking to see if he listened to what I said or not, and stepped over the mess on the floor on my way to the kitchen to get the first aid kit.

After three hours of waiting for paperwork to be over, we came here. In my experience, the administrative portion is usually done much faster, but it probably had something to do with every single cop coming in to see the Denver Thunders' QB sitting in their holding cell and a promise to my brothers that he would go out with them.

"Are you sure you're not going to get into trouble with the team?" I yelled to be heard over the running water as I washed my hands.

"Yeah, it's no big deal," he said, making me look up, and I found him leaned against the kitchen island. "The club has a bail fund, and if it's nothing serious, you just get a slap on the wrist, fined, and a game on the bench." He looked down to his injured leg. "Not a problem in my case."

"Did you get hurt?" The fear that the morons did some kind of damage to his injured leg while pulling him around my apartment, yelling at each other of who was going to get him first, was tearing me apart. Sure, the man did get on my nerves and frustrated the hell out of me, mostly because I couldn't kiss him and do other things to him, but I didn't want him hurt. He was doing such a good job. And he listened to everything I said he should do, earning my respect. I really hadn't thought he had it in him. It was bad enough that he got that angry-looking cut on his forehead as they shoved him out of the way when the cops came.

"Are you sure you don't want to go to the hospital?" I asked, biting my lip. I didn't get it before when I read or heard of a woman biting her lip, but now I found myself doing it every time I was near Jason.

He dragged his gaze from my lips to my eyes and shrugged. "Yeah, it's for the best. Besides, it's just a cut, nothing major."

I looked at him for a second longer, and then went to my couch, and flipping it back up, I gestured for Jason to sit. As I was preparing the alcohol and wipes to clean and bandage his forehead, praying to God it wouldn't leave a scar…it would be a shame to mar his beauty…he gave one cautious look at the door. "You're sure they won't come back?"

"Who, my brothers?" I chuckled softly, pressing the alcohol-infused wipe to his head.

Wincing slightly, his hands reached out to where I sat on the coffee table and squeezed my legs. "Yeah."

"You don't have to worry about them. At least not for tonight. While you were in the cell and before I came to get you all out, I called my mom to help me deal with them." I gave him a small smile. "She knows the deal. I can't believe I'm saying this and that it's even possible for three grown men, but they're grounded tonight."

"You love them," he said like it was a surprise.

"They drive me nuts on a regular basis and have me contemplating manslaughter more than occasionally, but yeah, I love them," I said looking from his forehead to his face. "They're the reason I got into physical therapy."

I didn't want Jason to think they were bad people. They weren't; they were just too... playful. They were also the ones who were there for me no matter what, who helped me in any way they could. And they were my protectors. Granted, the protection I needed was from them, but still, they were always there for me. They were my family, and I wouldn't change a thing about them. The thought Jason would think they were anything less than perfect had something in my stomach coiling.

"What do you mean?" his eyes roamed my face, every few seconds dropping down to my mouth, making me lick them in response.

"Well, since most of the time it was just the four of us kids and Mom had to work all hours, I was the one who took care of them. And you've seen them, so it's not a big surprise there were lots of broken bones, scrapes and bruises, pulled muscles, and so on. And every time they went to therapy, it consumed me, and I couldn't stop watching how they twisted their ankles, wrists, and everything to get them to work properly again."

"Then why not go into medicine?" he squeezed my thighs, his thumbs drawing small circles on the inside of them, making it hard to think.

"Honestly, I didn't have the patience for such a long time to be in school. I wanted to start living my life the moment I could and get the hell out of that house. And there's also the fact that I can't stand the sight of blood."

Just the memory of my brothers' failed attempt of giving themselves piercings on their brows and noses in our kitchen had me shuddering. It wasn't a pretty sight, and by the time we got to the ER, I was covered in so much of their blood the nurses called security on me, convinced I had killed someone. Or the time they came to my high school to scare my boyfriend into respecting me, only to end up fighting and beating each other up as to who would be the first to talk to the *little punk*.

"What do you mean get out of the house?" he continued with his twenty questions, still distracting me with his wicked thumbs that were going higher and higher up my legs, and I had to force myself not to flex my muscles in response.

"You picked up on that, didn't you?" I smiled even though there wasn't anything funny about it. I knew I shouldn't give him so much personal information, but after last night, he deserved it. And honestly, there was just something about him that made me want to give him everything. My whole being. I didn't want to think too much about it, because I was afraid of what it could mean. "Things at home weren't very... good," I said after a slight pause. How could I explain this to him without it sounding horrible? "My dad got killed in a car accident. A drunk driver lost control and swerved into his lane." The words started to come out automatically, like I was reading a grocery list, not even thinking about it.

"How old were you?" he asked as he leaned slightly toward me.

"I was four, Carter was six, Chace eight, and Max the oldest was ten." The day burned itself into my memory, and the sight of my mom kneeling down in front of the open door, her forehead pressed against the tile, and an officer trying to

get her to stand back up while she cried still haunted my
dreams.

"Anyway." I got back to my story after shaking my head to
chase the image away. "She had to take two jobs after that.
She had three growing, rowdy boys and a girl who still
needed food, clothes, and a roof over their heads in spite of
her world crashing down around her. It was difficult, and
she did her best, but three years later, she came to the
decision she just needed somebody to help her. And
honestly, I think she was lonely. She missed my dad, and
even though she tried to hide it, I could hear her crying
herself to sleep most nights. So, she married Nate who, as it
turned out, was and is a complete asshole. Sure, he helped
her financially, but basically, she just got one more person
to take care of." I was so lost in telling him my life story
that I wasn't even aware I started tracing his arms with my
fingertips. "After we were all moved out of the house, one
day, I caught her crying and looking at my dad's picture,
and I had enough. It took some time, but I convinced her
that she should divorce him. Unfortunately, it's become
almost a second job for all four of us to screen the men in
her life, since she started dating again." Which reminded
me, I had to call Max and see if he knew anything about her
new guy. Dammit, I've been so lost in Jason I forgot all
about it. "What?" I whispered when I focused on him again,
my fingertips freezing in place on his arms when the look
on his face penetrated my mind.

"This," he muttered right before his palms cupped my face,
pulled me to him and his lips covered mine.

Chapter Six

Jason

"Coming," I yelled, limping to the door.

I couldn't believe how nervous I was, but after last night and that kiss, the only thing I was absolutely sure of was that I needed Rory even more than I first thought. Listening to her softly telling me about her life, her brothers, and her mom, my plans about asking her out on a date and taking things slow, flew out the window. As I listen to her quiet words and watched the sorrow and love mix on her face, I couldn't help myself. I intended to hold her, to give her comfort and to take the hurt away, at least for a little while. But when she bit her lip, and I was half certain she didn't even know she did it, before she looked up at me asked, *What?* there was one thing that I could do. And that was to kiss her.

At first, when I pulled her to me and finally had the chance to taste her, she froze, and I was sure she would wrench my hands off her and throw me out. Just as I was about to pull away, apologize for my stupidity, and beg her to give me a chance, she melted under my touch, and a small moan she tried to trap, fought its way out through her sealed lips. The moment I heard the muted sound, I licked her upper lip so she would open up and let the sound flow into my mouth. Gasping, she opened her mouth slightly, I seized the opportunity and invaded her mouth with my tongue so I could have one of my dreams come true.

She was even more exquisite than I imagined. Battling with me for control of the kiss, she soon climbed on my lap, trying to push my tongue back into my mouth with her own. Her little hands on me drove me wild. I knew her touch from therapy; I even came to crave it on any day, but this level of need for her, surprised me yet again. I couldn't help myself. I couldn't stop. I pulled open her shirt, sending the buttons flying everywhere, and almost ripped her bra in my frantic need to see her. I tore my mouth from hers, gulped, and looked down. When I had the answer to one of the questions tormenting me daily, all I could do was swallow the saliva that almost started to trickle out of my mouth. Her nipples were pink on their outer edges and the firm tips were purple.

"Fuck me," I could feel the words scratching my throat as I half growled, half moaned. Giving in to the primal need that was swimming in me, I took one of her tits in my hand, watching closely as the other nipple turned darker.

Her hand cupped my face and yanked it up to her. She kissed me, taking advantage of my surprise by pushing her tongue in my mouth and then gliding it teasingly over mine. Growling, I took back control and plunged into her mouth when her hands pulled at my shirt to get to my skin, yanking it up, and she went right for my chest, making my eyes cross and roll back in my head when her blunt nails scratched the skin on my pecks.

"Rory," I panted, unsure what the hell I was going to say.

I knew we needed to stop, but when she didn't say anything and just leaned down a little to lick and bite my neck, squirming in my lap, all coherent thoughts went out of the window.

I took one nipple between my thumb and finger, rolling it slowly then pinching it and watched as Rory opened her mouth and whimpered while her eyes closed slowly. I was about to take it into my mouth when on the last roll she started to grind on my dick, making my aching cock weep. I knew I was seconds from losing myself in her, seconds from getting all of her, and when she whimpered again, I came to my senses and circled her waist with my hands, stopping her.

"Why are you stopping?" she asked between hard breaths, her hands gliding over my skin, her face still in my neck, her hips fighting my hands and trying to grind down on me once more.

I hated myself at that moment.

"Rory, baby," I gulped, praying to God what I said next wouldn't mean I lost all the chance I had with her. "We need to stop."

"What? Why?" she looked at me, her face a mix of confusion and desire.

"Because I need you to know I'm not just looking for a fuck."

Jesus, I couldn't believe the words coming out of my mouth. What guy in his right mind would stop a hot little thing like Rory? But as I watched the little crease form between her brows then a look of total horror washed down her face as she tried to get off me, I knew I did the right thing. I didn't want this look to greet me in the morning or to lose her as my therapist...and that would certainly happen if we carried on. Better for us to clear the air now than for her to run out on me later.

"Listen to me, Rory," I grabbed her hips again and shook her a little as she still tried to get away, pulling at ends of her shirt, trying to close it at the same time. "I don't want to *just* fuck you. I want all of you." I could see she was shutting the door firmly on me. *That's okay,* I thought. *For now.* I'd get to her.

She was mine. She just didn't know it yet.

"I think it's better if you go now," she whispered, not looking at me.

Fuck!

Did I just make a mistake?

"Please, go," she repeated, now standing in front of me, looking at the floor.

I sighed, hoping to everything that's holy that I didn't just blow my only chance with her. Taking her hand in mine, I squeezed it to get her to look at me and when I saw tears swimming in her eyes, I walked her to her front door.

"Look at me," I cupped her chin, pulling her face up when she wouldn't give me her eyes again. "We are going to talk about this. But for now, you need to know that I want you. And that I respect you. That's the only reason I put a stop to what was going on tonight. I don't want you to think I only want one thing from you." I leaned down and kissed her mouth that dropped slightly open during my little speech. I smiled to myself when that dreamy, unfocused look came back into her eyes. "I want all of you, Rory. Sleep tight, baby," I whispered, and with one last kiss, I turned and did the last thing I wanted to do.

I walked out.

~~*

"What the fuck do you want?" I sighed when I saw it was Curt standing at my door.

I could happily go one more week without seeing him. Or a year. Either way would be fine with me. When Curt said nothing, just gave me one of his smug little smiles that had even me shuddering, I open the door wider and went to the kitchen island to check if Rory's coffee was still hot and if I had enough donuts for her. I couldn't help but chuckle when I remembered the look on her face a few days ago, before our kiss.

After a particularly draining day for both of us, since my muscles were cramping all day, I heard Rory's stomach growl in response to my hissing threats about how I was going to fire her. She tried to hide it, but the coloring of her cheeks were a dead giveaway that she was embarrassed by the involuntary sound.

She was so beautiful and cute at the same time that I couldn't help myself and I blurted, "Want something to eat?"

I knew the moment the words left my mouth that I was playing with fire. All morning, the visions of her bent over the table where she had me sitting, then lying down played havoc in my mind. But I didn't want her to go just yet. I wanted to spend a little more time in her company.

"Umm...sure." For about five seconds, we stood opposite eachother, neither one of us moving a muscle. "Are you going to feed me or stare at me all day?"

She quirked a brow at me. I shook my head, partially to chase away the stupor her answer had given me, partially to

47

shake the sudden images of our lunch being pushed to the floor and her spread wide on my table. As I gave her the plate with broiled salmon and vegetables, I had to remind myself that no, I didn't want her. I hated her. She was, sadly, off limits. Or so I was still telling myself at the time. Hoping it would work and all those fantasies would stop.

"What the hell is that?" the demand came as I leaned over her plate on the island to squeeze the lemon on her veggies. Maybe I stepped over some kind of line? Maybe she wanted to prepare her meal herself?

"I'm sorry," I started to apologize for... well, I didn't even know what, but when I looked up I saw her eyes wide and a look of complete horror all over her face. "Are you okay?"

"What is that?" she repeated, now pointing at her plate.

"It's salmon and steamed veggies," I said slowly, "It's lunch."

"You eat that for lunch?" Now her wide eyes were aimed at me, and I felt something in my gut clenching.

"Yeah, it's in my diet," I whispered, absorbed as the look of horror vanished and a new one, a soft one, entered her eyes.

"Oh, you poor, poor thing," she patted my hand that was near her plate. "C'mon, let's go," she stood up, went for her things, and then started to go to the door.

"What?" I asked, that thing in my gut now trying to stop me from breathing.

I didn't want her to go. Damnit, I wanted her all to myself, just for a little bit more. And then, I would not be thinking how things should have gone while I was under another cold shower.

"It's your cheat day. We're going for burgers," she said like it was something we did all the time and I forgot.

She was almost jumping up and down on the spot the moment the word burgers left her mouth. I didn't like fast food. I enjoyed my diet, but I didn't tell her that. I went to her where she stood by the door, took my keys, and, through a smile, said, "Let's go for burgers."

From that moment on, she constantly asked me when my next cheat day was. She was determined to introduce me to all kinds of yummy food, as she called it. And every morning, she would taunt a donut or some kind of pastry under my nose. I didn't feel even slightly tempted, the big order of a burger with fries and fried onion rings followed by cake left me nauseous for the rest of that day, but learning the fact that my Rory was a food and sugar addict was amusing enough.

"We need to talk," Curt said, watching my hands as I fussed over the treats I laid out for Rory.

I needed everything to go perfect when she got here, so I could tell her she was mine, and then I would be able to actually cross some stuff on my list of things I planned on doing to her.

"About what?" I decided to get this over with.

It was easier to let Curt say what he came here to say so we can have peace later. Otherwise, he wouldn't get out and that would piss Rory off and ruin my plans of a fun private afternoon.

"About your contract."

Looking up I could see Curt had now gone to the couch and was sitting on it like he owned the place. Shit, he was going to drag this out.

"What about my contract?"

"I think you should reconsider signing a new one with the Denver Thunders."

The words that came out of his mouth had me seeing red. Was he out of his mind? If he didn't spit out and explain and do so soon, I feared I was going to kill him. I didn't have the patience for Curt today. Actually, no, I didn't have the patience for him at all anymore. And not ever if he was coming to my home with this bullshit.

"What?" I hissed, rounding the island and coming to stand in front of the coffee table. I watched Curt brush off an imaginary piece of lint from his tie then spread his arm wide on the back of the couch.

"I have a few new offers for you. Better ones. Generous ones," as Curt was talking, a slow, calculating smile spread across his face. "Ones that would make you a very rich man and take you closer to home."

"I don't want them. Tell them no. I'm staying with the Thunders."

"Now, look here. Don't be like that. Did you hear what I said?" the smile was no longer present. Now, there was an undertone of rage hiding under Curt's normal mask.

"I said no," I repeated.

"Listen to me," Curt stood up, pointing a finger at my chest.

"I said no!" I roared.

My whole body was twitching, fighting between staying in place and charging at Curt. How could Curt be so stupid? He knew how much the Denver Thunders meant to me. He knew how hard I worked all my life just so I would be where I was now. A starting QB for the Denver Thunders. And he wanted to take it all away from me?

"Is everything all right?" the soft question came from my left.

Rory was standing just inside the door, a nervous look on her face, ready to get out if needed.

"Yeah, baby," I sighed, pushing my hand through my hair, blowing a deep breath out, trying to calm myself a little and going to her. "Could you do me a favor?" I had to actively remind him to speak softly, when all I wanted was to beat the shit out of Curt for even suggesting the insane idea. When all Rory did was nod, I reached out and squeezed her hand. "Could you please go to my room and wait for me there? Curt and I have a few things to discuss." She looked from me to Curt and, nodding again, she squeezed my hand back in support then went and did what I needed her to do.

"Baby?" Curt sneered when the door to my bedroom closed behind Rory. "Is she the reason you're passing up this golden opportunity?"

Checking one last time that she was inside and couldn't hear any of this, I stalked over to Curt and got in his face.

"From the moment you signed me as your client, you knew what I wanted. You knew, and you still know how hard I worked for it. You know what my plans are regarding my career. And you also know the only team I want to play for is the Denver Thunders." I shook my head, unable to believe what was happening. "If you ever come to me with a crazy idea like that…If you ever even suggest I should leave all I have here behind, just so you can get more money out of me, you're going to find yourself penniless. Remember, we too, have a contract. And as I remember, I made you put in that you'll ask me before any decision is made and you'll listen to what I want. *What I want*, Curt. Not how much money there is to get, not how far you think it could advance my career. You knew from the moment you approached me that I wanted only one team. And you also know that if I find out you didn't do as you're supposed to, I can not only get rid of your ass, but you also have to pay the penalties. You thought I was just some stupid jock, but I've proven to you again and again that I have a brain in my head. So, don't do anything stupid, my friend. Don't make me fire you, Curt," I turned around, done with him, my intention now on getting to Rory. "Now get out of my house."

Still fighting the anger that was coursing through me, I opened the door and found Rory sitting on my bed. How could Curt be so fucking stupid? He knew how much this meant to me. And yeah, all he saw in me was a paycheck, since he demanded fifteen percent. Curt should know better though. My father added a stipulation in the final deal that even though Curt was my manager, he still had to consider what I wanted. He should be jumping at the chance to make everything I wanted to happen, happen. He should look for my benefit, and not his own. Why would he be so stupid as to go opposite of what was negotiated, of what they both signed?

And to suggest Rory had something to do with me choosing to stay? Sure, she was beautiful, she was smart, and she was funny. Whenever I was with her, nothing else had a place in my life. She was my only focus. She was mine, damnit. And nothing else mattered. Fuck, she was the most important thing in my life, and I couldn't stand the idea of leaving her, let alone actually doing it.

I needed her by my side.

So, yeah, she was a huge reason. Fuck, when the hell did that happen? When did Rory become more important than even football? *I don't give a fuck*, I thought as I slowly walked over to her not wanting to scare her. The only thing that was important was to fucking finally let her in on the play of things. To let her know she was mine.

"We need to talk," she stood up, watching me come in the room.

"Yeah, we do," I managed to push out over the lump in my throat. Fuck, I didn't even recognize my voice.

"You," she started to no doubt spew some shit about last night's kiss, but I didn't let her. I had no interest in hearing what she was about to say, since I knew it was a lie, she tried to convince herself of. She wanted me as much as I wanted her.

"I'm going to kiss you now," I whispered as I came to stand in front of her, leaving barely an inch of space between us.

And I did just that.

From the moment my lips touched hers, a current started to fly through me making my pulse go sky high. As I touched my tongue to her upper lip, she let out a small moan, opened her mouth, and let me in without any coaxing.

Fuck yeah, she was mine.

"Do you know how much I think about your lips?" I murmured a second before I plunged my tongue inside her mouth, not giving her a chance to answer, exploring every inch of it. Drinking from her.

My hands went from her neck, down her side and found the hem of her shirt and, pushing under it, touching her soft skin, they went up, taking the shirt with them.

"Do you know how many times I've wondered how soft your skin is?"

Reaching the edge of her bra, I swiped its cups with my thumbs and moving my hands up again, I pushed her shirt up and over her head. Throwing it away, I looked at her, barely able to stop from tackling her to the bed. There she was, standing before me in nothing but her leggings and black sports bra.

Fuck, she was a vision. A dream in the flesh.

Reaching out, I slowly dragged my knuckles from the base of her neck, her breaths coming rapidly, mimicking mine, over her breastbone to her right tit, watching goose bumps chase my fingers.

"Do you know how much I think about your tits?" I mused, not looking away from the nipple trying to break out of the cup. "How perfect they would be?" I continued in my musings and pinched her through her bra, rolling the nipple between my fingers, making Rory gasp in response. "What your nipples look like…how they would taste?" I leaned down and took a nipple in my mouth, tasting cotton.

"Jason," Rory whispered, bowing her back to give me more.

I pushed her bra out of the way and finally tasted skin. Cupping her breast, not waiting even a second, I went right back, and bit then licked her nipple.

"Jason," Rory moaned, her knees buckling, her hands now at my shoulders.

Not breaking contact but instead taking big pulls and alternately teasing her with my tongue, I pushed Rory on the bed and lay on top of her. Letting it go with a loud pop, I switched sides and gave the same attention to her other tit.

"Candy," I murmured.

Instinctively, I knew she was losing her patience when her hands dove under my T-shirt, and scratching the skin on my back with her little nails, she tore it off me. My focus was solely on her, her hair a disaster from thrashing her head all over the bed, her lips swollen from mine, her breaths coming fast. God, she was beautiful. As I watched her, I trailed my palm down her stomach to her thighs.

"Do you know how many times I've imagined your pussy while I was under a cold spray of my shower?" I gave her a cocky smile when I saw her eyes go wide. Half expecting her to push me off, I reached into her panties, touching only soft skin. "Are you wet for me, baby?" I whispered, leaning down to lightly kiss her lips. "Have you done the same? Have you touched yourself thinking about me?"

I was sure my cock was going to explode if I didn't bury myself in her soon.

"Yes," when she whispered her surprising answer, I lost all control.

Kneeling down on the floor, my frantic hands came to her pants and I tore her leggings and panties off, not stopping to even check if I shocked her. She spread her legs open, granting me with a view of pink perfection.

"Christ," I growled, reaching in my back pocket with one hand, taking my wallet out, then a condom. My other was pulling open the buttons of my jeans, freeing my hard dick. I tore the wrapper open and rolled it on, never looking away from Rory's pussy. All the while, Rory was impatiently shifting on the bed, opening and closing her legs, teasing me with this twisted game of peek-a-boo.

"Hurry," she whispered, looking at me down her body.

I reached out, my palms going to her knees then up her thighs, spreading her legs wider. I came to stand over her, and I whispered the last, most important question, "Do you know you're mine?" just before I slammed into her in one swift move.

"Fuck," I hissed when she started pulsating all around me. If she kept that up, I was not going to last.

"Move," she demanded through her hard breaths.

"Not yet," I grunted as her muscles flexed. Christ, if I did, I would come in a second.

"Move, Jason." She circled my waist with her legs, her hand going to my neck, bringing her lips right to mine, her other hand on my shoulder.

Opening my eyes, all I could see was my Rory, all I could smell was her, and all I could feel was her soft skin and wet silk. "Are you mine, Rory?"

"Yes, Jason," she moaned as I moved a little.

Pushing my hand under her, I tilted her ass and started thrusting. I wanted to take it slow, I wanted to explore every inch of her body, I wanted to let her know how much I wanted her, and how much I needed her. But as her moans and whimpers teased my ears, as her muscles started squeezing my dick harder and faster, I got lost.

"Rory," I grunted when she squeezed me like a vise, threw her head back, and opened her mouth as she came.

Bucking into her five more times, I pushed my face into her neck, smelling her, and gave over to the most intense orgasm of my life. Sometime after, I didn't even know how long I stayed buried inside her like that, she started to lightly scratch my back, almost purring as she felt me kissing her neck.

"Are you okay?" I whispered between kisses, not ready to let her go just yet.

"Yeah," she sighed, circling her arms around me, giving me a hug with all her limbs, and reminding me I was giving her all my weight and was probably crushing her in the process. Going up on my elbows, I looked down at her.

"God, you're beautiful."

The sweet, shy smile that made an appearance on her face was like a punch to my chest, knocking the breath out of me. I knew without a doubt that I would do anything for her smiles, but this one, the one that let me know just how much she let me see her, that she gave herself over to me completely, was something I would die to protect.

"You wanted to talk to me?" I quirked a brow at her, not wanting her to realize how much she had let me in and snatch it away.

Her palms came to my face and, pulling it down, she kissed my lips lightly before she pushed me back. Her smile huge, she said, "You're cleared for practice."

Chapter Seven

Rory

"Oh, God," I whimpered, seeing the image in the mirror.

I was bent at the waist, my hands on the white marble of Jason's vanity, my lips red going on purple and bluish in some places from Jason kissing me brutally the moment I stepped out of the shower. My hair that was once secured in a bun on the back of my head so I wouldn't get it wet in the shower was now falling down in all directions, some of it caught on the sharp, short spikes of Jason's hair at the side of his head. I barely reached his collarbone when he was standing up, but he bowed his head deep into my neck, making sure we touched everywhere. He was cocooning me, his chest flush with my back, bowing into me. I watched in the mirror as one of his hands cupped my breast, the fingers bringing me to the edge of insanity, his other arm around my waist, holding and preventing me from falling or impaling myself on the vanity. At the same time, he was pulling me into him, onto his cock. His muscles flexed with his every thrust into me. The slight tan of his skin complemented my porcelain flesh. We were the polar opposite, yet we fit perfectly.

"Hurry, baby," he muttered into my ear and went right back to nipping the skin of my neck.

"God," I moaned when once again, I took in the beauty that was reflecting opposite me.

"Babe, let go," he grunted.

I wanted to; I really did.

But what he was doing to me, how he was holding me, and those fingers of his that were now pulling me harder, had me holding on with everything in me just so I could prolong the feeling of him.

Him all over me, him inside me.

"I can't," I panted. "I need...." I didn't finish telling him what I needed, since I didn't even know what that was. It didn't matter, because Jason did.

I watched transfixed as the arm he had clamped around my waist loosened, his palm trailing along the skin to my navel then going down.

 Right at the center of me.

"Jason," I moaned. And when his thumb did a delicious little swirl, I lost the sight of us.

I let go.

The climax that tore through me was so glorious I had no other choice but to close my eyes and throw my head back where it collided with Jason's shoulder. It was magnificent.

"Thank fuck," he groaned as he stopped thrusting and started to glide. His tremors only managed to bring me back up to the peak.

I reached back with my arm, my palm going over his head, his short hair tickling, pushed my face closer to him, smelling his hair, and I hummed in pleasure. Feeling his hands start roaming my body, I was stunned at how good it felt, how right.

But most of all, how familiar it was.

I knew if there ever came a time when I wouldn't be able to have it anymore, to have him, I would miss it like crazy. We were together for five weeks, and this was how deep he was already rooted in me. And yet, every day, I was waiting for something to happen that would take him away from me. I told myself I was being silly, that nothing would happen, but unfortunately, there were signs that marred the perfection that was this past month and told me otherwise.

After the first time we were together and I told Jason he was clear to practice, the smile that spread across his face was that of a kid at Christmas.

The words barely left my mouth before he leaned down, gave me a hard kiss, then jumped off and said, "Get dressed. It starts in an hour. We're going to be late."

I was confused and a little alarmed at the sudden change, but even more curious about the fact that he apparently wanted me there. Sure, I had clearance with the team, since I had to give him his cortisone shots, but he didn't know that yet. "You want me to go with you?"

"Of course, baby," he said, turning just his head and giving me a wink over his shoulder. "Why wouldn't I?"

"I don't know," I didn't know how to explain it.

One moment, I was just his therapist; the next, he was kissing me or I was kissing him and then we had sex. Mind-blowing sex, for sure, but still. And now, I suddenly got access to all corners of his life. I was fully prepared to talk to him and pass him on to another therapist, my reputation of sticking through with a patient be damned, because I wanted him more than anything. I even had a speech prepared to recite before I jumped him and demanded he fuck me.

Apparently, we could do both.

Seeing him almost fully dressed, I put my butt in gear and got ready, making sure I had the shot before we went out the door. It was only slightly weird going into the locker room full of males in various stages of undress, but Jason took care of that by covering my eyes and bellowing, "Hide your junk! My girl is in the room. Let us through."

He guided me to the smaller room that upon opening my eyes drool practically trickled down my chin, since it was every physical therapist's dream. It had everything. And when I say everything, I mean *everything*. The room was huge and brightly lit. Upon looking up I could see why. Not only did it had row after row of lights, it also had huge windows on the ceiling. Looking back in front of me, I let my eyes roam the exquisite place.

On my left were ellipticals, treadmills, and a corner with only rows of jumping cords and elastic bands. It was odd because football players didn't need to do much of cardio. They needed their energy to be explosive and not to have too much stamina and lean bodies. Also, in front of every machine there was a TV mounted. I guess, the owners didn't want their players to be too bored while running. On the right were every station and machine with weights in every size and weight that probably ever was invented. And down the length, in the middle of the room were five big, comfy tables with stations safely tucked under them containing bands, bandages and ointments. I felt saliva pouring in my mouth upon seeing the room. And my palms started itching, wanting to glide over every surface.

Jason chuckled at seeing my dazed look, threw his bag into the corner, dropped his pants and shoes, and jumped on the table closest to us. "C'mon, baby, you have to get me ready for work. You can perv on the equipment later."

After the shot, a quick rub on the needle prick, and taping
his joint up, he leaned down, gave me that dizzying kiss
only he was capable of, and murmured, "Give it ten more
minutes. The locker room will be empty by then and you'll
be able to walk out unscarred by those monsters."

And then he was off.

It was entertaining seeing him this excited, since I hadn't
had a chance before, because from the moment I met him,
he was in a bad mood or angry. Sure, there were times when
he smiled and let his giddiness come out, and I did my best
to make that more frequent, but there was always worry
underlying it all. After waiting fifteen minutes, I was
contemplating how to sneak onto the field to watch Jason
practice and watch his muscles flex, when I remembered I
had clearance. I got a pass to every corner of the stadium.

So off I went.

Standing by the sidelines and watching guys be… well,
guys, one of them separated from the pack and came right
up to me.

"Hey, we haven't formally met," he offered me his gloved
hand, and I reached out and shook it. "I'm Logan. You're
Rory, right?"

I knew him, kind of. I'd seen him in passing while going to
or leaving Jason's apartment. Once, he even barged in while
I was in the middle of stretching Jason.

"Yes, Rory," I confirmed.

"So, you're Harris' new girl."

"Umm..." I didn't know how to answer that, since I didn't know what I was to him. We still hadn't had a chance to talk it out.

Suddenly, Logan turned to me and pushed his helmet so the face guard rested on his forehead. All the teasing that was in his tone was nowhere to be found. "Jason is a great guy. He really is," he said, looking sideways like he was checking something.

I looked that way too and saw Jason in deep conversation with the coach, his head bowed down, nodding in agreement, his hands on his waist while the guys were running around them. The next second, his head shot up. He looked right at me and smiled a smile that clearly stated he missed being there and was happy to be back.

"But…and sorry to have to tell you this…just be careful with him, Rory." The timbre of Logan's voice had me turning in his direction and losing sight of Jason. His eyes were watchful and full of regret. For some reason, he was warning me. About what, I wasn't sure. "I like you. I just don't want you to get hurt." And with that, he gave me a fast grin, pulled his helmet down into place, and ran off.

By the time Jason was done for the day, I was so turned on that the only thing I could think of was testing the durability of the table in the medical room and forgot to ask him why Logan would warn me off. Logan didn't once, in the times I saw him in passing, mention the stuff he said to me during that first practice or even try to warn me again that day. He was always happy, made everyone around him laugh, and was sometimes flirtatious. As with all the girls in his vicinity, the same with me. But every time I saw him, he would give me a small, sad smile. I didn't know what to think about it, so I just pushed it aside.

The other weird thing that was happening, unfortunately
every day, since that's how often he was at Jason's place,
was Curt giving me the side-eye and asking the same
question over and over. "You're still here?"

I didn't get why he would ask that, since he knew Jason's
therapy wasn't over, except somehow, I knew he meant it in
the context of my new role in Jason's life. I so badly wanted
to tell him off, but the moment he stepped over the
threshold, Jason would simply tell him, *Not going to
happen*, not even looking at him. Sometimes, Curt would
stay and do nothing except follow Jason with his eyes like a
hunter would watch their prey. Other times, he would get
red in the face, ask me that freaking question, then turn
around and leave. I didn't know what all that was about, and
I wasn't sure if it was my place to even ask, but it was clear
something big was going on between the two. I just knew
that after he left, it would take Jason at least an hour to lose
the grim look and shake off the anger.

Another thing that threatened to burst the bubble we were
existing in was the fact that Niles went from cornering me
in the clinic, to sending flowers with cards, in which he
asked, like a true gentleman, when I'd finally give up the
pretense and let him fuck me, to texting me at all hours of
the day, and once actually showing up at my door.
Unfortunately for him, Jason was at my place, and the
moment he heard Niles asking to come in so we *could
finally get to business,* his words, he came to stand behind
me and threatened to beat the shit out of him if he didn't
leave immediately. I'm not proud of the fact, but I would
have let him. I wouldn't even call the cops. After Niles left,
Jason made me tell him the whole story and demanded
I report Niles at work, which I did. Even I couldn't bury my
head in the sand any longer and convince myself I could
handle him. Something needed to be done. When I refused

to move into Jason's place, he then called Max and told them everything.

Needless to say, if I wasn't with Jason, I was with one of my brothers or Mom.

There was also the fact that women kept showing up at Jason's house in various stages of undress. One even stood at the door wearing nothing but panties and high heels. I kind of wanted to know how she got there undressed like that without ending up in a police station for the night, since I didn't see a purse or coat on the porch when I opened the door.

One in particular was very persistent. She didn't even care who she'd find when Jason told her Logan wasn't there. All she cared about was getting her rocks off by a football player.

Mindy.

She was drop-dead gorgeous.

Long, chocolate-brown hair, sultry brown eyes, full red lips, and a velvet voice. Not to mention she had a body of a model, one that gets paid a lot and women all over the world drown their sorrows in ice cream looking at her picture in a magazine, because they know they'll never look like her, have a body like hers, or dress like her. Their husbands probably imagined her while they were sneaking off to the bathroom for a jerk-off session. I opened the door one day, wearing nothing but the white towel wrapped around my body, and as she looked at me from the slits that were her eyes with a sneer pulling at her top lip, in a sweet voice I singsonged, *Oh, sorry, you caught us in the shower. Logan's not here, and Jason is busy giving me the business, if you know what I mean.* I said that last part leaning toward

her with a wink and then closed the door in her stunned
face. I may have also been wearing a shit-eating grin
through all that on my way back to Jason, but that wasn't
important.

 But there were also the times when I was sure Jason was a
man who I could fall in love with. Actually, I was falling in
love with him. And that scared the shit out of me. I realized
that when I put my foot down and, two weeks ago, said,
"Enough is enough! We need to go out, back into the world.
This practice, sex, practice, sex routine is getting ridiculous.
I love your body; I love watching it move, especially if it's
moving while inside me. But I need to eat, and those gross
things you swear are healthy and nutritious are not food.
And I need to have dinner with my mother and meet her
new man. And I just decided it's your cheat day. So put
some clothes on, stop distracting me, and let's get a move
on."

Jason didn't put up one single protest to my demands.

It probably had something to do with the fact that I let him
eat me out on the kitchen island and fuck me while bending
me over the table before we left. But we did go to meet my
mom's new man. And Jason bought flowers for her. And
coffee and cake for me.

Also, he was giving it his all to hide the fact that he was
Sebastian's, mom's new boyfriend, number-one fan, since
he was apparently some hot shot in the managing athlete's
business. Jason told me he couldn't even get a meeting with
the man, let alone get him to represent him, before he settled
with Curt.

"I thought managers hunted players down, not the other way
around," I mused, getting lost in the way we were strolling
in the evening, Jason holding my hand, with the streetlights

shining on each side of us and the stars twinkling over our heads. Just like any normal couple.

"Usually, but Sebastian is such a legend. He takes care of his clients, and I mean he *takes care* of them however they need, as long as they're not doing anything that could damage their career or something that's illegal. He has a waiting list," he said, pulling me to him, wrapping his arm around my waist, and finally kissing my hair, not even missing a step.

"Hmmm..." I hummed from the sheer beauty that was the moment. "I'm impressed you didn't try to get him to sign you."

"I would never do that to you. Tonight, wasn't about me. It was about meeting your mom and spending some time with your family," he replied as if it was nothing, when in fact it meant everything. "Besides, I'm not even on his radar. And I don't want him to represent me, not now."

"Why?"

"Because he's a part of your family now, and I don't want anyone to think I used the connection."

Yeah, he was shaping up to be perfect.

Every morning, coffee would be waiting for me, the steaming cup sitting on the edge of the island, no matter whose place we were at, and a pastry treat. And even though Jason followed his diet like it was the sacred law or something, he never complained that I detested it, never demanded I just try to like the healthy food he ate or that I eat my junk food or whatever I was gorging myself on in another room. He even cooked it for me. He did try to sneak something healthy in, and I ate just a little so he wouldn't feel bad. He even got with the program for me and had a cheat meal here and there. Last night, Jason went out with my brothers, who were on cloud nine all day getting to hang out with other players and have some guy time. My mom kept me company, and Sebastian called frequently to check on us, even though it was unnecessary. I haven't seen or heard from Niles since I put in a complaint. He got fired, and after encouragement from almost everyone, I started the process of getting the restraining order. It was good to spend some time with my mom; she was finally smiling freely, and there were no shadows in her eyes. She was happy, and it was a sight to see.

But I missed Jason.

I wanted to be with him, lazing around on the couch and watching a movie or working out in my gym. I didn't care, as long as I was with him. I practically ran to the door when there was a knock, my mom's chuckle trailing me, only to open it and see Jason hanging by his arms on Max and Chace's shoulders.

Max scowled at me and accused me, "Your man is a lightweight. He got three beers in him, and halfway through the fourth, he started falling down."

Like I was somehow guilty for it. They carried him into my room and placed him on the bed before they left. I was pulling Jason's shoes off to try to get him more comfortable, when he bent at the middle, sitting up, and caught my elbow, pulling me to him.

"Rory, my sweet Rory," he smiled drunkenly, astonishing clarity washing across his face, and he muttered, "I love you."

Then, he dropped down, passed out and left me completely stunned. So yeah, fuck yeah, he was shaping out to be the perfect guy, and all the evidence told me that the cocoon he wrapped us in was made of steel, and nothing could rupture it.

Chapter Eight

Rory

"You still ignoring what happened last night?" Jason whispered in the skin of my neck. He wrapped his arms around me and did what I thought was impossible, pulled me even more into him. "Or this morning?"

He was asking about the *I love you* that fell from his lips. I convinced myself that I misheard him last night, that he didn't say the words.

While I was brushing my teeth, he changed the routine this morning, and instead of putting the coffee mug on the island, he carried it to my bathroom and put it next to the sink.

"Hurry up, baby," he said, looking at me in the mirror. "We need to get to my place so we can do the therapy and get me ready for tonight's game."

I nodded, looking back at him. I was probably just as excited as he was for his first game after the injury.

We had a meeting with his doctors, coach, and the owners of the team a few days ago, and all agreed that as long as Jason stayed in his place after he threw the pass and not go running around the field, tackling or pushing through the other players, he could play. He wasn't happy about that, since he was probably the only QB in the league who tried to play all the positions and didn't care he was only supposed to throw the damned ball, but he agreed. Until he was fully healed, to prevent a repeated injury, he'd play "like a granny," as he called it.

"Okay, hurry, I'm going to get dressed so we can go," he leaned into me, kissed my hair, and whispered in my ear, "I love you."

He didn't give me a chance to tell him I loved him, too. He just left the bathroom, and by the time I managed to get myself into gear and ready, he was gone. I was too nervous to tell him I felt the same way.

"Hmmm..." I hummed, turning my head toward him and pushing at his chin with my forehead so he had no other choice but to lift his head and look at me. "I have no idea what you're talking about."

"Oh, nothing important," the small smile he had on his face was filled with nervousness. "Just the fact that I told you I love you. Twice."

Looking at him, I felt like something in me released. My heart was beating fast, but it was light. My hands that were behind his back, around his neck and head, started tingling now for a totally different reason. And my legs became like jelly.

"I love you, too," I whispered, looking deep in his eyes. As the words came out of my mouth, his eyes started to get darker until they almost looked black.

"Fuck, we don't have time," he growled, pushing the air from my lungs as he squeezed me, his eyes that were becoming even darker now trained on my mouth.

"Time for what?" I whispered.

"For me to fuck you again," he leaned down and gave me a light kiss. "I love you, baby. Now, I have to let you go so

you can go into the other room to get ready. If I don't, we
won't come out for three more days."

He did warn me, but the swift way he did it had me reaching
to the cold marble to prevent myself from falling down.
Still, I didn't try to hide the huge grin I had on my face
when he looked back over his shoulder seconds before he
pulled the door closed.

~~*

"I doubt that you'll be here ever again, or that you'll even
last until the next game the Thunders will play, but you
need to learn the rules," the nasty voice stopped me as I was
coming out of the family box at the stadium.

It was after we finally made it out of the apartment, after we
came to the stadium and I pushed the last cortisone shots
into Jason's ankle, taped him up, and got here to watch the
game. The game was over, and I was on my way to the
players' exit to wait for Jason. They won, and we had a lot
to celebrate. I looked behind me to see four women standing
in a straight line, their arms crossed over their chest, hips
cocked out, and each wearing a matching sneer on their
face. Behind them, Mindy was lurking, looking between
them and me, and an ugly smile spread across her face.

"I'm sorry?" I asked. What the hell?

"You need to learn the rules," the blonde one said.

"Most importantly, you need to learn the hierarchy," the one
with jet-black hair finished.

I looked them over. They were all kitted out like they were
on their way out to a club, dressed to the nines, hair big, and
makeup thick, prowl ready.

73

"Oh" was all I could say.

They ignored me the whole game, only occasionally throwing dirty looks my way. But when I chanced one more look Mindy's way and saw she settled in for the show, I knew this showdown was her doing. They were her friends, or they tolerated her enough to believe all the bullshit that came out of her mouth. The only problem was, I had no idea how it involved me.

"Yes," the redhead, I think her name was Autumn, continued, taking a step toward me. Clearly, she was the leader of this little pack.

"The first row?" she asked, even though she was telling me, pointing at the row with her finger. "Is for the wives only, second for the fiancées, and third for the girlfriends," she finished, focusing back on me. "The disposables like you have no place here, but when you manage to weasel your way in, you stand by the wall, only coming to the bar if you absolutely need it, and then back to the wall, and not sit in the first goddamned row. The few of us who are wives worked our asses off to get our men, took a lot of bullshit, and ate a lot of shit just so we could hold the position. So, it's rightfully ours. You do not come in here and disturb all that."

Dear God, they were lunatics. I would laugh if I didn't see she was dead-serious. I had no idea how she could believe in half the stuff that came out of her mouth, let alone convince herself it was okay to live by that...that code. What woman in her right mind would put up with something like that? If what she hinted at was true, did she get she was talking about chairs at a football stadium? I knew she probably got other perks in her life, and for her sake, I hoped it was enough and she got exactly what she wanted, because I knew I couldn't live like that.

But still, right this second, she was trying me to put me *in my place* over chairs.

"Jason Harris?" she asked and shook her head at me, fake sadness coating her tone. "Not gonna happen, honey. He doesn't know what he wants or needs. Our girl Mindy here," Autumn jerked her head back. "That's the girl who's gonna warm his bed for a long time, who's gonna get his diamond, and who's gonna put the gold band on his finger in the end." The sneer came back. "Not you."

She took another step in my direction and all I could do was gawk at her for the sheer stupidity and insanity that was coming out of her mouth.

"In the unlikely event that the impossible happens and you get a repeat performance, you need to dress up to the standard," once again, she looked at me from top to bottom.

I had on my *worn so much they were almost white* jeans, but they were my favorite, and when Jason saw the cuts on the knees and the one at the top of my right thigh, his eyes had gone dark and he shook his head, muttering *Not enough time*, before he turned and stalked to the door. White Converse on my feet, and a red T-shirt, which Jason had signed in the locker room, right under the words ***Love you*** on the outside and ***I'm going to fuck you later*** that he wrote on the inside. It was sweet, it was funny, and it was definitely sexy when he wrote it. I promised myself I was going to frame it and hang the shirt in my bedroom.

"No more of this…this…I don't even know what to call those rags you're wearing. As long as you're near Harris, you represent him and this team, so you need to act and dress accordingly," she started to walk to the door but stopped when she was next to me. "But don't come back if you know what's good for you. Leave him to his girl," she whispered, and one by one they passed me and walked through the doorway, leaving me alone to watch Mindy wink and wiggle her fingers at me. I was so shocked that the only thing I did was turn around and walk out. All the way through the hall, my steps echoed around me, but I barely heard it. What was with all the warnings against being with Jason? First, Logan and his looks of sorrow; now this, what did they call themselves, WAGS, wives and girlfriends of sportsman?

When was Mindy ever involved with Jason?

I knew he knew her before, but she was trying to get Logan and tie *him* down. They hooked up a couple times and even made out when we were all hanging in the bar after practice one night, before Logan got bored and cast her off. She tried getting to him by coming to Jason's place, looking for him, and that was only because she didn't know where Logan lived. At least, that's what Jason told me. All the guys thought it was funny that Jason lived in a small house, and they frequently came over with girls. That way, the girls didn't know where they actually lived, and the guys got entertainment when Jason had to fend the women off his property. Sure, it'd stopped since we became an item, but I knew some of the guys weren't happy about it. Especially Logan and Dylan.

Was it possible Mindy and Jason were together?

When were they together?

When did they break up?

Did he tell her he loved her, too?

The first tear that fell jolted me, and I quickly wiped it away. I didn't want anyone to see me cry, especially not

those vultures. Was he only playing me? What did he think
he would possibly get out of it? By the time I came to the
mouth of the hall, right where the players were coming out,
the streaks that my tears were leaving on my face were more
than obvious. I looked up and was met by the smirks of the
foursome that ripped me apart, and I was so focused on
them I unfortunately didn't see another snake coming right
at me, ready to strike.

"You're still here," the snide comment was a punch to my
already bruised heart. I looked to Curt, wanting to tell him it
was probably the last time he would see me, but he didn't
give me the chance. He took a menacing step toward me
and hissed, "You need to cut Jason loose. Because of you,
he's passing the opportunity of a lifetime."

"What?" I whispered through cold and going on numb lips.

"Oh, he didn't tell you, did he?" the evil smile warned me to
brace, but I wasn't smart enough to listen. "He's got offers
from all over the country. The most lucrative one coming
from L.A., which we both know is right around the corner
from where he grew up. Now, he won't admit it, but he
wants to take it. The only thing keeping him here is you and
your cunt." He took a step back, and just like the WAGS did
ten minutes before, he looked me up and down. "I don't
know if it's sweet enough to pass over twenty million
dollars, but I sincerely doubt it just by looking at you. So
back the fuck off, lose that ironclad grip you have on his
dick, and you and your pussy need to disappear from Jason's
life. Am I clear?"

"You're fired," the barely restrained rage coming from
behind Curt's back surprised us both.

Turning around quickly, Curt put his hands at waist level,
his palms pointing to the ground, and he was moving his

arms up and down like he was pushing the air down. "Now, look here, Jason. I don't know what you think you heard, but, Rory and I…we were just having a little chat. Nothing more. I just wanted to check in to see how your recovery was going."

One of Jason's brows had gone up, "So, the fact that I just heard you telling Rory about the contracts I refused several times and spewing shit that she needs to leave me, not to mention calling her a cunt, was all my vivid imagination?"

"Now, I never called her a cunt."

That was not the way to go. With a jerk, Jason threw his bag from his shoulder and had a hand wrapped around Curt's throat, pushing him into the wall in the blink of an eye. I watched it, but still I didn't see when he did that; it was so fast.

"You ever come back or near Rory, I'm going to kill you. You hear me?" If I were in Curt's place I would nod frantically, but the man just looked at Jason and patted at his wrist like one would a child on the head. "Do not *ever* come back. I don't want to see you. I don't want to hear you." Pushing Curt farther into the wall, which I thought was impossible, he finished on a scary whisper, "and I especially don't want you to even breathe around Rory, let alone talk to her again. You got me?"

Curt glanced at me sideways, but quickly looked back at Jason when he shook him a little and slammed him back into the wall. He was now turning blue in the face, and his palm that was patting Jason's wrist started to claw at it.

"You got me?"

He gave one last stubborn look before he wheezed, "Yes."

Taking a step away, Jason released him, and Curt crumbled to the floor, rubbing his neck and sending me a hateful look that had fear sneaking up my spine. Not even sparing him one glance, Jason bent, picked up his bag, threw it over his shoulder in one fluid move, took my hand gently in his, and pulled me away from those horrible people. Right to his car. On our way out, I couldn't help myself, and I turned over my shoulder, raised my hand and gave the WAGS a nice little wave and a smirk. The sight of their stunned faces was a nice perk, too.

I knew I shouldn't have; I knew it wasn't my place. And I also knew his answer had the power to destroy me. I kept telling myself to keep my mouth shut, to not ask anything and just gather my things at Jason's house and go home. This was too much. The things that were said to me today hurt too much. And I wasn't sure if I wanted to find out the truth.

Still, I did.

I opened my fucking mouth.

"Are you leaving Denver?" I wasn't even sure if he heard, my voice was so soft.

"What the fuck?" Jason whispered, looking away from the road to glance at me. "Of course not. Why would you even ask that?"

"Curt," I said in answer, which it wasn't, but still.

"Don't listen to him. He's just a snake looking for his next big payout," Jason dismissed everything that happened and shut down the car, exited it, and said, "let's go inside."

I was so wrapped up in my head I didn't even realize we were at his place. Okay, maybe I got it wrong. Maybe what Curt said to me was a lie and he was just trying to get me to leave Jason. Why? I had no idea. But still, there was one other issue that was swimming around my mind, torturing me. Mindy.

"And what about your girlfriend?" I asked his back as he let us in his home.

"What?" he whispered, looking back at me, the muscles in his back flexing. In fact, his whole body was turning to stone right before my eyes.

I didn't take it as a good sign, and if I was smart, I would just say nothing and get out. Unfortunately, I wasn't all that bright, as it turned out.

"I hear you have a girl who's going to wear your wedding ring in the future, waiting for you to have some fun or whatever, and then you'll go back to her to ride happily into the sunset." Walking past him, I ducked my head and swiped at the traitorous tears that had started to leak again.

"You're fucking with me," he closed the door and followed me with his eyes. "Tell me you're fucking with me."

I said nothing, and when I started to gather my stuff from all over the place, he came to me.

Pulling at my elbow, he turned me to him, "Rory, tell me this is some kind of joke."

Again, I said nothing and just looked past him.

"How in the actual fuck do you think that's even possible? Who told you that?"

When I kept my silence, he shook me, my head snapping
back, and at the sound of pain coming out of my mouth, he
released his grip and took a step back. I could see he was
shaking with rage. Barely holding it together.

"It was those bitches, wasn't it? The shit-for-brains plastic
Barbies," swallowing, he took a step toward me, but I
stepped back. His eyes zeroed in on my feet and he tried
again, only for me to take another step back. His eyes came
to mine and I could see fear mixed with anger dancing in
them. "I can't believe you would ever believe them. I would
never do something like that. I thought you knew me better.
I just fired my manager because he was a dick to you, for
Christ's sake!" he yelled. When I stepped back again, he
took a deep breath and closed his eyes when releasing it,
visibly calming himself down. "Don't be afraid of me. I
won't hurt you. In fact, I won't even touch you. But listen to
me, Rory. I'm not that kind of man. I would never cheat on
you. I would never take advantage of you."

"What about your career?" I whispered. There was a big
possibility that he was leaving Denver. Maybe not this
season or the next, but that was something that could
happen in any given moment.

"Fuck my career!" he roared, leaning toward me, his hands
balled into tight fists. "I don't care anymore. The only thing
I care about is you. I even told you, I love you. Do you
know how many women I've ever told that? Do you, Rory?"

I just shook my head, too scared and too shocked to do
anything else.

"None. Not fucking one. You're the only one who got those
words from me. Fuck me, but you're the only one who
evokes that feeling in me. For you to think I would be a
piece of shit who would cheat on someone, let alone on you,

then when I get my rocks off go back to some skank that's happy to wait until I dicked around on her? And she is a skank, Rory. I told you I met her before I met you, so I know the game she plays. I'm a professional football player. There are always women trailing behind, trying to get us to notice them. It's the same in any sport. But I never had anything to do with her. It was offered; I won't lie. I just didn't want the one who was offering it." The look of sheer repulsion stretched his mouth. "I wasn't a virgin when you met me; you know that. You also knew I didn't get my balls in the traps those women call hands. I never had a thing with one of them or the ones in their circle." He looked to the side, shaking his head. He closed his eyes and, obviously coming to some kind of decision, he looked back at me, "and yeah, fuck yeah, you're the reason I said no to those contract offers. But you're only one of the reasons. All my life, all I ever wanted was to play for the Denver Thunders. I worked my ass off for that. And now that I've finally got it, I'm not going to throw it away for more money. I have more integrity than that. And if, and that's a big if, they decided to release me from my contract, I still wouldn't go." He was breathing hard. I could tell he wanted to come to me, but he stayed rooted to the spot.

"Why?" I whispered, new tears coming down my face. I had a good idea, but I still wanted to hear it coming out of his mouth.

"Because you're here." The veins in his neck pulsed. "You've become more important than anything. Even football, even my future." I took a tiny step toward him. I wanted to hold him so much it physically hurt. He stopped me with his hand raised, "don't come near me, Rory. I'm so fucking angry and I know if you come near me, I'll just fuck you and try to forget this ever happened. But, I can't. I can't understand how you could believe them. If you don't

believe in me…in us," he sighed, shaking his head. "I just...
can't."

He sighed again, looked down, pushed his hand in his hair,
and I watched as his shoulders slumped down. After a
moment, not even sparing me a glance, he turned and went
into his bedroom, softly closing the door. But that soft click
pulsed in me from head to toe. I stood there not moving, and
I cried. How was it possible that we went from that sweet
place he had us in only a few hours ago, to this cold
existence? How couldn't he understand that I just wasn't
able to dismiss all that was said to me today? Coupled with
the regretful looks and warnings from Logan, it all fit. It all
made perfect sense. And all those fights between him and
Curt were clear now. All his bad behavior. His mood swings
whenever Curt was near, his impatience when Mindy would
show up at his door. Still, even when she said she was
looking for Logan. And when we told her that Logan wasn't
there, she asked for any player that came to her mind. Only
recently had she started to hunt down Jason.

And he was always with me, spending almost every second
of the day near me. I haven't once seen him sneak around
with his phone or take off without explanation. With all that
running through my head, I knew I still shouldn't have done
what I did.

I loved him.

And I wanted him.

And I needed him.

He was my everything.

Sure, maybe I had trust issues. Maybe I needed to start
listening to my heart. I should have listened to him and

came back tomorrow. I should've just gone home. Maybe
I'd be spared the pain later on. Maybe, but who knows?
Still, I wiped my face and went to him.

Chapter Nine

Jason

"Jason?" Rory's sweet whisper tickled my ears, but even that wasn't enough for me to look up from my bent position of staring at the floor.

Softly, I could here her coming toward my bed, where I was sitting down. Still, I didn't look up, I couldn't look at her.

Not now.

After the last month, I was sure she was mine completely. I was sure she believed in me...in us. My biggest fear was that she would crack under the pressure that being with me would bring her. I was scared shitless when that first picture of us taking a walk was taken and the press, blogs, and numerous fans started sharing it on social media, asking who the mystery woman was.

But she didn't say anything. Didn't act any different.

That was the following morning right after we had dinner with her mom and Sebastian. Besides the picture of us walking together, the fuckers got it just at the right time. In it, my arm was around her, pulling her to me, my eyes closed while I kissed her hair. Both of her arms were around me, her eyes also closed, but she had a little satisfied smile on her lips and her head was at an angle, almost like she tried to hide it. I was torn between wanting to kill the fuckers who took it or find them and thank them. She was so extraordinarily beautiful in that picture. They also printed a picture of us, her mom and her boyfriend laughing and clinking our glasses together at dinner. I couldn't remember what we were toasting to or even laughing about. It didn't matter. Sebastian was almost as famous as any athlete, so of course the questions came pouring. I walked on eggshells all day, but again, she just took it in stride.

So, I finally relaxed.

I was happy. I was in love.

I thought nothing could break us now. But I foolishly forgot about the wives and groupies, and I didn't even think about Curt. They got to her. For her to so blindly assume they were right, that what those snakes were whispering in her ear was true, I couldn't help but feel betrayed. I risked everything for her.

Curt even went to the team owners behind my back and asked them to consider releasing me from my contract early so he could pursue other teams, other opportunities, a better paycheck. It was pure luck that they decided to talk to me first. To say I was shocked that the fucker would go to that length was an understatement. I did everything but beg them not to sever the contract. It took some convincing but, in the end, they believed me, that it was only a misunderstanding and not some play to wring more money out of them. They did say they'd have to think about what their next move would be and about the next season. But they also did say they would hate losing me, and after promising one more time, I had no intentions of leaving the Thunders, they shook my hand smiling. Thank fuck I nipped that in the bud.

"Jason?" she asked in that timid voice.

God, how I hated the sound of that. I never lost my shit like that before. I went to great pains to push down the urge to rip apart anyone who threatened my future, only to lose it in front of the woman who *was* my future. The scared look she had while I raged in the living room was something that would haunt my dreams and weigh heavy on my soul for the rest of my life. I never wanted to see it again., and I was scared I would lose it again if she didn't back off.

"Not now, Rory." my voice scratched my throat. "Just...leave me alone." I still didn't trust myself enough that I would stay calm.

She didn't do as I asked, of course, she didn't. Instead, she knelt in front of me, her hands going to my legs, where she pushed them apart and shuffled on her knees, coming closer between my thighs.

"What are you doing?" I asked when her hands started roaming the muscles, her fingers putting pressure on the knots in them and loosening them up.

"Trying to relax you. We don't want a repeat injury," she said in a monotone voice, her sole focus on her job.

Of course, she came in as the physical therapist, not as my girlfriend. She was getting paid for it, and she was good at her job. The best. The irony was not lost on me. So, it was only logical she would see it through to the end.

"You can do it later," I muttered, trying to brush off her hands.

She put her palms flat on my legs, dug her fingers in, and demanded, "Look at me!"

When I focused on her eyes, I could see they were still wet from her crying, full of regret, but, thank fuck, the fear that was in them moments ago was nowhere to be found.

"I'm sorry."

It was sweet. I wanted to take her apology and say it was okay. But it wasn't. She gave up on me at the first hurdle.

"Rory," I sighed, pushing all the way up to sitting straight.

I didn't know what to say, but I didn't get a chance to figure it out. She moved her hands, dragging them over my pants, going up, right to my belt, and started undoing it and the zipper.

"What're you doing?" I grabbed them to stop whatever she had in mind.

"I'm saying I'm sorry," She wiggled a little, and when I let her go, she went right back to her task.

"Not now, Rory," I grabbed her by her shoulders. The sneaky woman pushed her hand in my boxers with one hand and grabbed my dick, which started to go hard the moment she knelt on the hard floor.

"Yes, now," she didn't look away from my eyes as she started stroking me.

I wanted to kiss her. I wanted to lose myself in her. I wanted to forget this day, no, this afternoon. I wanted to forget that this afternoon ever happened, but it wasn't that easy. She needed to start trust me, trust in what we had. Shifting, I tried to dislodge her hand from my cock, but she winked at me, pulled my dick out, and in the next second bent her head and took me in her mouth.

"Fuck, Rory," I hissed, gave up all protest and leaned back on my arms when I felt the perfection of her hot little mouth, my eyes rolling back in my head. I couldn't help but to flex my hips just a little. Testing her. She accepted it like a pro, moaning around the shaft, sending a thrill up my spine. She released my dick with a pop, her saliva stretching from the head of it right to her bottom lip.

She swiped at it with her tongue, looked at me, and repeated, "I'm sorry."

I just looked at her. I wasn't able to speak. She stood up, opened her jeans, and dragged them and her panties down her milky legs. When she kicked them out of the way, along with her shoes, she went back down on her knees.

"I can't," I started to say, but she stroked me again, giving a little twist and a thumb swipe at the head, robbing me of every coherent thought. "Baby," I grunted my stomach clenching.

"I love you, Jason," she breathed then went right back to lick and suck at my dick like it was an ice cream cone.

One hand under her mouth tracked the movements of it, the other alternating between massaging my balls to swiping between her legs. I reached out until my hand came to her head to fist her hair. I flexed my hips again while I held her head in place and got the same reaction from her as the first time. And when she spiked the tip of her tongue in the slit on its head, I had enough and pushed up to sitting and reached to pick her up. Her knees came to the bed on either side of me. She took hold of my dick like she was afraid it was going to run away from her and tried to position herself so she could sink down on it. I held her fast and wouldn't allow it.

"What happened today can't ever happen again, Rory," I told her in a serious voice. I needed her to understand her opinion was the only one that mattered. As long as we were together, nothing could touch us, "I love you, baby, and I can't lose you."

I would do anything to have her look at me like she did this morning, like I was some miracle that walked this earth. I would make her feel safe with me again. Safe in the knowledge I wouldn't ever hurt her. Safe in knowing I wouldn't ever betray her. Safe in giving herself completely once again to me.

"You won't," she promised, her eyes dazed from lust, not fully knowing what she was promising. But I knew, and even if that made me a bastard, I would hold her to her promise.

Only when she leaned down and kissed me did I loosen my grip on her hips and allow her to slide down on my cock. Lying back down, I enjoyed the show as Rory rode me to her climax. And with only a little of my guidance, she did the same for me. I knew, even if she did, I would never give up on her. No matter what, I would fight for her, and I would demand that she keep her promise.

"Don't stop," she moaned, still wanting more, even after I ate her out. She sucked me off, and I tackled her to the floor in the bedroom to fuck her.

"You're wearing me out," I half muttered, half chuckled, gliding in and out gently from her tight pussy. I was whipped. I needed to get to bed and get some shuteye before getting on a plane tomorrow morning.

"And you're a liar," she took my earlobe between her teeth and pulled.

For the last two weeks, she slowly came back out from that hiding spot she retreated to after what those bitches and Curt said to her. Every day, she would give more of herself back to me. Still, there was fear lurking behind her hazel eyes, and sometimes it leaked out, marring the perfection. I hated seeing it, but I knew only time could show her that she could trust me again.

"After we made each other come several times, first when I ate you out, and then when you sucked me off, while fingering yourself until you came, you almost drove me to insanity or a heart attack while I watched." Expected her to blush and retreat again. Every time I teased her, she had the same reaction, retreating into herself until I managed to pull her back out. When she opened her mouth and sassed, I was shocked as shit.

"Don't you dare be lying on top of me, with your cock still hard in me, I might add," the last part, she said in a deep tone, trying to imitate me. Which only made me laugh, and that had the consequence of her squeezing my dick until I groaned, "and say you didn't enjoy the show."

"Far from it, babe. Not only did I enjoy it, but it's going to get a repeat performance as soon as I come home, and it's going to become a staple show in this household," the moment I hinted to the fact that I was leaving, even if it only was for two nights, the green that was in her hazel eyes started to dim, and she looked to the right. I kissed her neck and whispered, "I'll be home before you know it, honey."

I didn't want to leave, but it was my job, and I had no other choice. When she still didn't look back at me, I shook her a little, and only then did she sigh, right her head, peck me on my lips, and signal for me to get off her.

"Nothing's going to happen, Rory," I whispered, still not letting her go. She needed to understand I would never hurt her. I would tear my throwing arm off before I would ever do that. "I'm just going away for a couple days to do my job, and then I'm coming right back to you."

"I know that," she bit out.

"You've got to trust me," I sighed.

"I'm sorry. I do," she cupped my face. "It's only the WAGS I don't trust."

"Well, thankfully, they don't have a hold on me, and I can think with my own brain, so you can trust me."

She focused on my eyes, hearing the seriousness in my tone, "I know; you're right, and I do trust you," she whispered before she winked. "Now get off me so I can clean up and we can go to bed. Then you don't have an excuse as to why you didn't fuck me and make my coffee before leaving."

~~*

"I miss you," Rory whispered through the phone like it was some secret she wasn't supposed to tell me.

"I miss you too, honey," I whispered back, but unable to bite back his grin.

It was a good night. We had our game, we won, and now all that was left to do was go back to the hotel room and wait for daylight to come so I could board the plane and get back to Rory. Get back home. For the first time ever, I truly hated my job. My life path. I wished I didn't have to leave her behind when the team played the away games. Sure, she could have gone with me, as other PTs do with their players, but she had other patients and she loved her job, not to mention was determined to rise right to the top, so I didn't even ask. And when she had a meeting with the team doctor, it was too late to bring it up and see if she wanted to go with me. She assured me the doctor was more than capable of doing what was best for me and that she gave the medical team traveling with the club all the instructions needed. So, I bit my tongue and left her behind.

It was what it was, and I couldn't turn my back on it. I had a plan, and I was going to make it a reality. I only needed to make sure Rory was with me every step of the way, and if that meant her flying out with me on the away games, it was okay. Because this sleeping without her shit was not going to happen again. And since all her patients were professionals, I was sure all of them would understand if she went away for a few days.

"How's your ankle?" she asked around a yawn.

It was late. By the time the bus took us from the stadium to the hotel and we had dinner and a drink in the hotel lounge, it was after midnight. I needed to let her go to sleep.

"It's okay," I said, walking past Logan and Curt, who were in some kind of standoff. My guess, Curt fucked over another one of his clients. Ignoring Curt, I gave a chin lift to Logan and went to the elevators.

"No tension, limping, or anything like that?"

"Stop, baby. I'm fine. You did a great job. Besides, it's been a week since I was cleared for full-on play, and still I listened to you and didn't *run around* as you call it," tagging the button for the elevator with my knuckles I looked up at the red numbers going lower over the elevator door.

"Hey, man," Logan said as he came to stand next to me.

"Hey." I focused back on my call to Rory. "Okay, baby, I'm going to let you go now. I'm standing in front of an elevator, waiting to go up to my room to try to get some sleep."

"Okay," she sighed. "I love you." Every time she gave me those words, I felt them hit the center of my chest, and the sweet pain made the breathing a little easier.

"I love you, too. Sleep tight," I shut off my phone and put it into my jacket pocket.

"You want to have another drink?" Logan gestured with his arm to the lounge.

"No, I'm going to bed."

I was just about to step into the elevator when Logan asked again, shifting from foot to foot. "You sure?"

Before I could tell him to fuck off and go find someone else to drink with, a low whistle came from somewhere. Logan looked that way then back and with a grin said, "Never mind. Have a good one."

By the time I got to my room, all thoughts except sleep and Rory vanished from my head. That was until I opened the door of the room, only to find Mindy lying on the bed wearing nothing but panties and high heels.

Chapter Ten

Rory

The chime of my phone alerting me I got a message pulled me out of a very pleasant dream that had Jason starring in it. I reached out to the nightstand, not opening my eyes, and blindly tapped around it until I found what I was looking for. I brought the phone up to my face and nearly blinded myself when I engaged it.

It was a message from Logan.

It was also after three in the morning, so why he was texting me, I had no idea. He sometimes did that, texted me, but it was always during the day, and it always had a link to some funny post from social media or something along those lines. Tamping down the disappointment that it wasn't some sweet nothing from Jason, I touched the icon and opened it up.

It wasn't a text but a video.

Dread instantly filled me, since I could see the first shot was of some hallway. I wasn't in the mood for anything scary, but I pressed the play icon on the little square and watched the footage of Mindy coming out of the room, cupping her bare breasts, and sauntering in the opposite direction when the door slammed shut behind her. Whoever shot the video, slowly came down the hall to the door, so the room number was clearly visible, 531.

Jason's room number.

Jason's room.

I was still in numb shock when my phone chimed again, and exiting the video, I got back to Logan's text thread.

Logan: I'm sorry, sweet girl.

Logan: I told you to be careful.

Logan: I'm so sorry.

The three texts came one right after another in a second. I sat up, exited the messages, barely holding down the sob that started to travel up and out of my mouth, and dialed a number. I had to hold it together. I had to shove that image I just witnessed out of my mind long enough so I could get my stuff and go home, to safety…and there I could fall apart. There, I could let the hurt pour through and exit out of me in the form of tears. Not here. Not at Jason's place, where I didn't belong.

After five rings, the sleepy voice came. "'Ello?"

"M-Max?" I barely pushed through the tears that didn't listen and started leaking out of me.

"What's wrong?" his voice was alert in a second. I could picture him jumping out of his bed, scanning the room for threats as if we were still living at home and I had a nightmare.

"I-I... I need you to come to Jason's and pick me up," I wailed.

"What? Now?" The confusion morphed into anger. "What's going on, Rory?" Hearing my brother being angry for me at whatever was happening had me spilling everything to him about the incidents at the stadium and the fact that, that night, Jason scared me, but I was weak and still stayed.

Unfortunately, the fear of him betraying me, playing me, hadn't left me. Including the video I just got. Not even half an hour later, which was half an hour too long, as I was shaking from trying to hold in the hurt, I heard a light knock on the door and ran to open it.

"Thank God you're here. I co-" the words died in my mouth, seeing the person who stood there.

"Yes, thank God," Niles sneered. "You're a slippery little thing, Rory. But finally, I have you all to myself."

He took a step toward me. I instinctively took a step back and collided with the wall, essentially trapping myself. Niles slowly reached behind him, not taking his eyes from me, and shut the door, turning the lock. I watched, hopeless, as his hand raised when he did that and then came down toward me. The bad news was, the pain radiating from my eye and cheek matched the one that was in my heart. The good news was, I passed out.

Chapter Eleven

Rory

"He was here again today," Chace said under his breath as he walked past me from my kitchen to park his ass on the couch and wait for the game to start.

I looked that way, only to see the picture of Jason on the screen while his stats this season were rolling, and the commentator gave his prediction of tonight's game, my heart screaming in agony. God, he was beautiful. I missed him so much. I wanted beyond anything to be at that stadium, cheering for him. To get him ready for his game. To celebrate the win, he'd no doubt give his team.

And then to come home with him. To have him hold me.

And to chase away the residue of the nightmares that still sometimes tormented me.

But I couldn't have that. I was weak, and I was scared. It's been three weeks since Niles attacked me in Jason's loft. It was pure luck that I called Max to come get me and take me home. It meant Niles had only five minutes with me alone before Max showed up. He knew something was wrong when I didn't answer his call to tell me he was in front of the building, and when he came to the door and heard Niles's grunts, he didn't hesitate to break it down. He tore Niles away from my unconscious body and beat him to a pulp, locked him in Jason's bedroom, checked on me, and then called 9-1-1. In those five minutes, Niles didn't have time to do what he was clearly bent on doing. He wanted to fuck me but was firm while talking to the police through a bruised jaw that it was not going to be rape, just two people attracted to each other. And sure, I was playing hard to get, made him work for it, as he explained, but I repeatedly sent him looks and signals that were clearly telling him I wanted him.

No matter how much he told that tale, no one believed him, and he was currently in jail, awaiting a trial. Jason came to the hospital the next morning, but he didn't get into the room. At my request, my brothers stood guard in front of the door. I knew he would come, since I hadn't yet told him I had proof of him lying to me and saw Mindy coming out of his room.

"Get the fuck out of my way," his demand could be heard over the beeping in the hospital room.

Every muscle in my body hurt, my lips were split, and it was hard to breathe. Still, the moment I heard his enraged voice, I tensed. Niles went to town on me in the little time he had, so not only did I have bruises and one swollen-closed eye as a souvenir of his visit, but I also had cracked ribs and a sprained wrist from when he tried to drag my body into the bedroom. Guess he wanted to have me on the bed.

"No way, fucker," Carter growled at Jason. "Not only was she attacked in your home, which means you didn't care enough for her safety and left her unprotected with that sick fuck on the loose. You also betrayed her in the most fucked up way."

"Besides, Rory doesn't want to see you," Chase put in.

"Not after what you did in your hotel room," Max finished for him.

"What the hell are you talking about?" Even then, he was playing as if he didn't know why I would stop him from getting to me.

I knew my brothers were showing Jason the video of Mindy coming out of his hotel room by the silence. I sent it to them, because it hurt too much to talk about it. The one time I told Max what happened almost undid me, and in the end, I wasn't careful enough and opened the door to Niles without checking who it was, because I was so desperate to get out of there. Listening to the silence, watching in my mind as Mindy walked nearly naked down the hall, I was no longer just tense. Every muscle in my body turned to stone. At that point, I didn't know what hurt the most, my bruised body or my shattered heart. So, I took hold of the thingy the nurse explained that with one push would send the medication coursing through my body if the pain ever got to be too much to handle, and I pressed the button on top. I needed relief. Not from injuries, but from my heart shattering over and over, because that damn footage kept playing on a loop in my head.

"That's not what it looks like!" Jason shouted. "Someone set me up!"

"Sure, sure," Max muttered, disbelief ringing all around. "Still, you're not going in there. She doesn't want to see you."

I don't know how long Jason stayed in front of my hospital room, arguing with my brothers. The drugs started to pull me down, and I fell asleep. He came to the hospital every day in an attempt to see me, and when I got home, he came to my apartment, checking up on me, bringing food and sweets, sometimes flowers, other times coffee, and always asking if he could see me. When he was denied access to me, he would stand in that hallway, waiting.

There was one thing I didn't get. How did Niles find me? Jason's address wasn't a known fact. Sure, he had a lot of women knocking on his door, but that was only because guys kept bringing them there. I doubt one of them would tell anyone where he lived. Not because they respected his privacy. No, because they didn't want competition. Besides, none of them knew I was there that night.

That answer came later that first night in the hospital, when Logan came to see me, almost as frantic as Jason was. Standing by my bedside, my brothers scowling at him from the opposite side, he broke down and started crying.

"Hey," I whispered, patting his hand. "I'm okay, just a few scratches and bruises. I'll be all right."

But he just bowed his head, begging me to forgive him, hunching over our hands on the bed, his shoulders shaking between his ragged breaths.

"What for?"

I didn't get it. Why would I need to forgive him? He was the one who kept warning me Jason would do something like this. And when he did, Logan was the one who alerted me of it and prevented me from becoming a fool who would have everyone laughing behind her back.

"The video I sent you," he started when his remorseful eyes found mine. "It was a setup. Mindy wasn't with Jason even a full minute in that room. Two seconds after he got inside his room, he threw her out. I just waited until later to send it, so it would look like she was in there a lot longer after you two hung up."

"Why did you do that?"

"Curt," he shrugged, looking away, and I watched as shame washed over his face. "He told me if Jason took one of the deals that were on the table, I would be able to get a better deal from the Thunders. Get more money, better sponsors, and more offers. Jason's the star of the team; everyone knows it. The rest of us? We just grab any leftovers from the sponsors we can get. And watching everything be presented to Jason and listening to him while he bitched and moaned that it was all a distraction from the game, then shoving all that money aside, living in that tiny house, I was jealous. I wanted it all. So, when Curt came and told me he would make it happen for me if we got Jason out of Denver, I went for it. I didn't let anything stop me. Not even standing by his side at the elevator and listening to him tell you he loves you. I just didn't think something like this would happen." He looked back to me, swallowed hard, and whispered, closing his eyes. "I am so sorry, Rory. I'll do anything for you to forgive me."

I was so lost in the relief that coursed through my body, acting like a balm to all my aches and pains, that I frowned in confusion when Chace asked, "How did Niles find her at Jason's?"

I didn't get how Logan could know.

"Curt told him. He was hell bent on getting Rory out of the way, so he made his mission to know where both of them were at any minute of the day. He was paranoid that Rory would take him to Sebastian and help Jason get signed by him." He grabbed my hand and shook it. "I found out this morning. I promise you, if I knew what Curt was doing or what Niles wanted to do, I would have warned you. I would've stopped Curt. I wouldn't have gone through with his sick game."

I asked Logan to tell all that to the police. He did, but unfortunately, Curt claimed he had no idea who Niles was and that he thought he was just a guy from work, so when he told Niles where he could find me, it was only because Niles said it was work related and he couldn't get me on the phone. Since there was no evidence that what Curt did was in fact done fully knowing and understanding the situation, he was released. Though I heard he was losing clients and was not in such a good position. I was also ashamed I so easily believed in Jason betraying me. I wanted to tell him I was sorry, I missed him, and that I loved him.

But I didn't want him to see me like this.

And besides, we clearly didn't work. I had trust issues, over which I just couldn't get past. It was better that we broke up and went on with our lives. He didn't deserve me questioning his every move. He needed someone who believed in him a hundred percent. He just wouldn't hear any of it, or give up.

"Yeah, he spent an hour sitting in the hallway, waiting for you," Max picked up the bags of chips when I came near the couch, not looking away from the TV. "He would still be out there if he didn't have to go to the game."

I knew Max was right, since he sat in my hallway every day, most of the day. The bruises were fading, and with makeup, they were barely visible, so I was running out of excuses not to see him. I just feared that if I did, I would cave and wouldn't be able to let him go.

"Maybe you should..." Carter started to say.

They were trying to get me to talk to Jason for the last week, figure things out, and get back with him. From the moment they heard Logan's words in my hospital room, they started doubting the video. Then they went to him and demanded the truth. Since then, they were trying to help him however they could. Still, I stood my ground. It wasn't the fact that they were slowly but surely chipping away at the wall I built, all four of them, that had me tuning Carter out. It wasn't even the fact that a close up of Jason, in his standard position, head bowed, nodding, his eyes trained on the ground, hands on his hips as he was taking a step onto the field, was on TV. It was the fact that I couldn't see the blue strip snaking up his leg.

"I'm going to kill him," I growled, not looking away from the screen and putting down the bowl with the dip a little harsher than was necessary, sloshing the stuff over the edge and all over my hand and table.

"Who?" the three men sitting on my couch asked, but I didn't answer. I went right up to the TV and squinted.

"Please don't lick the screen. Please don't ruin the game for me," Chace groaned.

I ignored the big baby, turned around, and went to my bedroom then to my bathroom. Right to my box of tampons.

"Fucker, oh I'm going to kill him," I muttered to myself as I pulled out the four passes from the box.

 I planned to surprise my brothers with them, take them to a game and to meet all the players and tour the place. Something they've never done. In all that's happened, I just didn't have a chance, and I didn't want to come face-to-face with Jason. On my way back to the living room, I snatched my coat and bag and marched out, right to the door.

"Let's go," I barked to the three, who were trailing me with only their eyes.

“Where?”

“The game's about to start!”

“Are you serious?”

I didn't answer the questions that were fired at me in rapid succession, just flung the four plastic cards over my shoulder and left them dangling there, holding the blue and red ribbons. I could hear all three jumping to their feet and the sounds of them moving around, gathering their things.

“It's not that I'm complaining, because I'm totally not,” Carter was the first one to catch up to me, and he tried to snatch the passes away. “In fact, I think you're the best sister there ever was,” he said in a sweet tone, trying to get me to give him the passes. “But what happened to change your mind about seeing him?”

I was so furious I was barely able to get the words out of my mouth. He knew he needed to do it; I went to great lengths to teach him how to properly do it. And I explained the risks, in great detail, of what would happen if he didn't do it. And still, he ignored me.

“The fucker didn't tape his ankle.”

Chapter Twelve

Jason

"Sit your ass down back on that bench," the little growl I
could barely hear over the roar of the crowd made my heart
stop for a second.

I tried to look in the direction where it came from, but with
coach yelling in my face and the doc shouting his questions
in my ear, I couldn't see a thing. Shaking my head to clear
it, I tried to pull my focus back to where it belonged. In the
game. But, as it was for the last three weeks, nothing could
hold my attention anymore, not even my career. I didn't care
for anything, couldn't think of anything except the fact that
Rory didn't believe my and that she left me. How the fuck
had I managed to be stupid enough to fuck everything up so
royally?

"Harris, are you even listening to me?" the coach hollered in
my face.

I gave him an automatic nod, just so we could get this over
with.

"I'm going to fucking kill you."

There it was again.

Her voice.

It was filled with so much anger that I could barely
recognize it. God, did I missed her so much that I was
imagining her being angry with me?

"Why in the fuck did you think it was a good idea for you to sprint to the end zone? Haven't we discussed this shit already?" The coach was now looking at me like I was a moron who couldn't even tie his shoes.

"You didn't even tape your damn ankle. If you have a repeat injury, I'm going to break your neck, you idiot!"

What the fuck? I knew she told me the biggest risk came from repeat injuries, but to actually imagine her giving me a lecture now was a little bit over the top, even for me. God, I missed her so much. Nothing made sense without her. I didn't want anything if she wasn't by my side. I didn't care about anything except her. Not even football. That was why I didn't do something Rory tried to drill in my brain. I didn't tape my ankle, and I started sprinting the moment the receiver caught the ball. I just wanted the game to be over so I could go back to her place, sit in front of her door, and beg or wait for her to give me a chance to explain. It was only when my cleat was pulled off my foot and my leg shifted to lie on someone's leg that I looked down, prepared to tell whoever dared to manhandle me to back the fuck off. The sight of her hair all over the place, her cheeks flushed, her mouth in a straight line while she was twisting his foot, was beyond my wildest dreams.

"It took me almost two hours to get here the city is so full," she kept with the growling, her sole focus on my foot as her frantic hands put the tape on my leg. "And then you did something this moronic before I could get here."

I reached out and covered her hands, "Baby, stop." She looked at me.

If she could, I was sure she would spit fire right at that moment. I have never seen her so angry. And then it penetrated that she was here. She thought I would hurt myself, and she rushed to get to me. She was so beautiful, even with the bruises still slightly visible under her makeup. I reached out and gently touched her cheek with the tip of my finger, pushing down the rage that erupted when she flinched away. If I could, I would kill Niles for what he did to her. I did however beat the shit out of Curt, so at least he did get some kind of revenge for what happened to her, and I whispered still not believing it was true and not a mirage, "You're here."

"Of course, I'm here," she yelled at me, her face getting red. "You're acting like an idiot and putting yourself at risk."

She went back to work, and I burst out laughing. If I knew that was all it took for her to come out of her hiding place, I would have done it weeks ago. Fuck, I would purposely twist my ankle again if I knew it would get me a minute of her time. I reached out and gently cupped her face, aware of her bruises, and pulled her up until she was on her knees, so I could kiss her lips. With my lips still against hers, I opened my eyes.

"You're here," I repeated, unable to believe it even though I was touching her. It was a good possibility that someone tackled him, and I had a concussion. "You came."

We were so close that the only thing I could see were her stunned eyes, and I vividly watched as they started to go gentle. I felt under my palms when all her anger and fear melted away, and she relaxed her face.

"I'm here," she whispered.

"I'm so sorry, Rory. I'm so sorry for what he did to you," I rushed on to say, hoping she will let me talk. I didn't know how much time I had before she disappeared on me again, and I needed her to know the biggest regret I would ever have in my life was that I left her unprotected. And in my goddamned home. "And I promise you, nothing happened with Mindy. I threw her ass out the moment I entered my room," I knew if I didn't get it all out now, I wouldn't get a second chance to explain.

Maybe it wasn't the right time or place, but I needed her to know everything, so that we could move on. I was also living in a hotel. I put my house on the marked the moment I came back to Denver. Going so far that I got Dylan to take out all my stuff, because I couldn't go in there and see the place where Rory got hurt. I didn't trust my reactions, and if I saw what the place had looked like after Niles was done with her, I probably would have ended up in prison. Also, I absolutely refused to buy a new home without her. So, hotel it was. She once told me about her dream home. A farmhouse with a white picket fence, a huge lawn, and lots of trees. And I wanted to give it to her. To do that, I needed to guide us back together so she could pick out our future home.

"I know," I could feel her biting her lip under his.

"You know?" I pulled back and looked at her. Something in my gut started twisting again, and it had nothing to do with this urgency I felt.

"Yeah, Logan came to see me and told me everything," she said so low I had to read the words from her lips.

"Then why did you refuse to talk to me? Why have you left me?"

"At first, I didn't want you to see me all broken," she looked to the side, gulped, and then looked back at me. "And after some time, I knew I fucked up again. I didn't believe you.

Didn't believe in you. And you deserve someone who believes in you."

"But I only want you." How could she not see this? If it meant proving that to her day in and day out for the rest of my life, I would gladly do it. I didn't need her to believe in me anymore; I just needed her to give me the chance to prove it to her. "I don't care what you think I deserve. Nothing else matters but you."

"Yeah, you demonstrated that tonight," she tried to shake her head to admonish me, but with my palms still at her face, she couldn't, so she settled for a stern look she couldn't quite pull off with the small grin on her face.

"Rory, I love you," I all but yelled so she could hear me.

"I love you too, Jason," she shuffled on her knees to come closer to me.

"Promise you won't leave me ever again."

I wanted to tell her everything. About how I sold the house, the papers were signed just two days ago, about her needing to get out and find the house she wants, so I could buy it for her. I was still on rocky ground with the team; they weren't very pleased with the stunt Curt pulled trying to get me released from our contract, and I got called into a meeting again where they informed me they were thinking about doing just that. I have to admit it was disappointing to hear that after our initial meeting. But, I didn't object. They needed to do what they needed to do. I didn't think about it; I just thanked them for letting me know and left the office. I didn't even look at any of the offers. I didn't care. If they released me, it would mean the end of my career. So be it.

My life was in Denver.

Rory was in Denver.

And that meant I wasn't going anywhere.

I would simply find something else to do.

And even if it took me years, I would live in that hotel room, waiting for Rory to forgive me, and then take her to find us a home. For us. For our future family. I didn't have time for all of that right this second, so I made sure she knew I loved her, hoping it would be enough for her to stay until the end of the game, so that we could talk.

"I promise," the words barely left her mouth before I leaned in and kissed her. It wasn't a light peck on the lips. I went whole hog. It was slow and wet. It was also hot as all hell.

"Thunders, huddle!" Dylan roared so everyone could hear, standing behind his back.

My teammates jogged to where we were, Rory still kneeling, me sitting on the bench and they circled us, giving us their backs. As one, they all extended their arms back together, each holding a helmet in his hand, and one by one, the helmets clicked in place, right above our heads hiding the two of us.

"What's going on?" she asked, looking up to the helmets that hovered over us.

"The Thunders huddle," I explained, still holding her face. I looked up smiling and was glad to see even Logan's helmet hovered over. Logan tried to talk to me, but I still wasn't ready. I could barely stomach seeing the man on a daily basis and not give into the urge to kill him, since he was the one who helped with breaking Rory and me up. Swallowing the bitter taste that only thinking about it left in my mouth, I looked back to my girl. "They're giving us privacy, baby. In the last place you can expect to have it."

Rory smiled and kissed me again. This one was fast though, and just like the one before, it was also wet and hot as hell. She then pulled out of my arms, bent down, and started working on my leg. When she was done, she tapped the player nearest to her on his calf to indicate we were ready for them to go.

"Go win the game, QB," she bossed, kissing me on the cheek just as the huddle broke and everyone in the stadium could see. Which meant everyone cheered. "My brothers know about the passes now, and they expect the same for the Super Bowl."

I just shook my head, smiling, and grabbed my helmet from the bench. I stood up and walked onto the grass and giving her a wink over my shoulder, jogged onto the field to do as she said.

Epilogue

Rory

Ten years later

"Please, stand up and give a mighty applause for the best QB the Thunders ever had, Jason Harris. This is the last time we'll have him in this role. The last time his name will appear on the players list. After ten years, the best QB in the league has decided to put his helmet down, and even though he's not here with us today, I'm sure he's here in spirit. The Denver Thunders thanked Jason. You have been the best player and the best friend we could possibly ever ask for."

"We could have been there," Max whined, his hands extended to the enormous TV that was hung on the back wall of the house. "We could have drank in this energy. Damn, we could have even stood in the center of the field." His hands now at his waist, Max hung his head and shook it. "You wound me man," he muttered, not lifting his head up.

The chuckle that came from behind me still gave me goose bumps. I turned around, and my eyes found Jason's as I rolled mine and grinned. He was standing at the grill, the light smoke surrounding him, a beer held in one hand and his eyes that were aimed at Max through his whining and begging came to mine the second I turned around, and he gave me a sexy smile.

It was the first game of the season, and the last official one in Jason's career. He didn't want to be there. He decided he was going to retire last season, but the Thunders didn't want to announce it, hoping he would change his mind. So, they held off, and when it became clear he was determined, they had no choice but to do it today, without Jason there. We all were invited to the ceremony, but Jason said he spent enough time on that grass and was looking forward to watching the game from home. We still had our own little ceremony, but it was for family only.

Everyone was here, my brothers with their wives and kids, my Mom and Sebastian. Jason's parents, Dolores and John, Logan and his wife, Dylan and his, and Matthew. Jimmy was at the stadium, since he still played. I still couldn't believe my brothers found their wives and that any woman in her right mind would have them. Then again, I still had the bail fund, only these days it was used for their wives and me. They took every opportunity to rub that in my face, and no matter how many times I tried to explain it wasn't my fault, but they'd met their match in female form.

Ten years ago, after the game that I rushed to in order to tape up Jason's leg, Jason took me to his hotel room and told me everything. He then took me out the next day to look at houses. We didn't find one for a long time though. Even at the slight wrinkle in my nose, or me inspecting something too much, Jason took it as indication that it wasn't the home of my dreams.

In the end, he moved into my apartment, and five years ago, he bought this land and started working on building my dream home. Five years ago, we also got married. The only ones who were present were the people standing in our backyard today. It was a long road, one that was extremely rocky, but Jason did forgive Logan for what he did. It probably had something to do with Logan calling every day to check up on me, and anytime I needed to go somewhere or do something, he was always there to help. I still sometimes could see ghosts lurking in his eyes, more when he went through his painful gig with his wife, but they were becoming less and less visible. I tried to talk to him, tried to get him to stop feeling guilty, but he just said, "Give me that, Rory. I almost cost you and Jason your future, but most importantly, I almost cost you your life. I thought I learned my lesson, but as it is with life, it gave me one I will never forget. And in doing so, it gave me more of the understanding of how it felt, and honestly, I don't want to ever forget it."

After that, I backed off, but I still hoped he would stop tormenting himself with what was done. I watched him hug his wife from behind, his face tilted down to her neck and his eyes closed, I also understood he never would forget. He had a taste of that fear and hopelessness, and he didn't want to.

It took me almost a year to get Jason to sign a contract with Sebastian. He flat-out refused when I mentioned it the first time, saying he didn't want it; he would figure something out. Sebastian was family, and he didn't want anyone to ever have the thought of him using me and my connection to Sebastian. It took Sebastian to come to our home, sit Jason down and explain a few things. It was also after I called him and said I failed once again in reasoning with Jason.

"I'm a fifty-five-year-old man who didn't have anybody before I met Teresa. I built an empire but no one to leave it to. And then Teresa came into my life, giving me three sons and a daughter. And the daughter gave me one more son. Now, tell me, boy, who in their right mind wouldn't do anything possible to help their family? So, no more of this bullshit, no more refusing, and come into the office Monday morning and sign the damn contract, so we can get to business."

And that was that.

He went in, they signed the papers, and Sebastian made sure Jason played for only one team the rest of his career. The Denver Thunders. It didn't take long for Chace to start working with Sebastian, and surprisingly he was good at it.

"Mommy," the high-pitched squeal made me turn just in time to see Carter swinging Amelia, our four-year-old, up in his hands, over his head, and settle her to sit on his shoulders and walk my way.

The moment the words *I'm pregnant* came out of my mouth, Jason lunged at me, fucked me in our bed, and then pulled me out of it when we were done to drive here to tell him my vision. We got married the week after. We moved into the house that resided in my mind, which Jason made a reality, a year and a half later.

Amelia was a carbon copy of her dad in a little girl form. She was also spoiled rotten by every member of our family. But her favorite, besides her daddy, was her uncle Carter. I still couldn't believe he held such a huge secret from me, and it took me a long time to forgive him. But I totally understood why he did it. "Are we gonna play?" she asked, pulling on Carter's ears and bouncing up and down on his shoulders.

"Go easy on your uncle, princess, or I won't be able to work tomorrow," Carter chuckled, coming to me and pulling her down so I could take her.

"How dangerous is tomorrow's gig?" I asked quietly, searching his eyes for any indication it was indeed dangerous.

"It's routine," he dismissed my concerns. "Do you think I would jeopardize what I have now?" He asked the question he always asked when I started to interrogate him. And I knew he wouldn't, it was just that he held a huge part of his life a secret before it blew up in his face. "Besides, your husband holds me on a short leash."

Four years ago, Jason went into business with Carter opening a security agency that did anything and everything under the sun, thanks to Carter's expertise. Unfortunately, it meant Carter was a PI playing bodyguard. It did however bring him to the woman who was now his wife, and she held him on an even shorter leash, only allowing him to occasionally put himself in danger. The fact that he found her meant Carter stopped chasing that adrenaline rush and started to slow down, not that he would ever admit that.

"Mommy, let's play," Amelia whined, her little hands pulling my face to her.

"Okay, baby," I murmured, smiling. "Go get Daddy and let's play."

I put her down and watched her run to her hero and tug on his hand. I started walking in their direction, and we met halfway just as Carter whistled to get everyone on the lawn.

"You okay?" I asked my husband and rounded him and our daughter, who was in his arms, with my own.

"I'm perfect," he muttered, leaning down to me. "How are you?" he whispered. I knew he was asking about the morning sickness by the glint in his eyes. Two days ago, I shared the news we were going to have another baby, and we still hadn't told anybody, since we wanted to wait for the first trimester to pass and we were sure everything was as it should be.

I shook my head and gave him a small smile in answer but asked, "What are you going to do now, QB?"

"He's gonna play!" Amelia shrieked before Jason could open his mouth.

"I'm gonna play," Jason repeated, his eyes dancing.

Five minutes later, we were split up into two teams, and as the whistle from the TV could be heard, I watched my husband as he threw a football for the last time in his professional career right in our backyard, cheered by the crowd that was miles away.

The End

The adventures of Ryan family will continue with story of Max and Skylar

Acknowledgments

I hate this part. I'm terrified that I'll (unintentionally) forget someone.

So, I'll start from the start.

Zulfa Cupido, woman you're a godsend. I cannot nor will I ever be able to express how much all the things you did mean to me. The way you cheered me on, never letting me stop and even start to think about just throwing in the towel and calling it quits, is beyond words. Yeah, it left me speechless. Thank you!

Sue John, you are the best alpha, beta reader and all the other letters in the Greek alphabet there are. Your gentle nudging and cheering, not to mention every time you've read a chapter sending me a message of I LOVE IT, kept fueling me on. Thank you!

Sean Hurdle, not only do you spread the word about my books, but you also took on an enormous task of formatting this little gem of mine. I can't say thank you enough… But, Thank you!

To my readers, you stick with me with every new story that comes out. I love whenever you reach out to me just ask a question or talk about some part of the book that you just can't get out of your head. It's the reason why I do this. Thank you so much for letting me know that I am doing a good job. Thank you!

And as always, last but most important, to my husband and son. Sven, you leave me speechless every time you ask if I have to write today and then just scoop up our baby boy and go entertain him, even though I know you're exhausted and all you want to do is sit on the couch, eat and snuggle (with me...LOL). Thank you so so much, I love you to the moon and back. Thank you!

Baby boy, you're just the perfect human being. You're the force that drives me day in and day out. If I ever come to wonder if in life I did one great thing all I have to do is look at you. Thank you!

That's it, that's all I have to say...for now.
All that is left is…   HVALA SVIMA!!

About The Author

Ana Balen was born in Zagreb, Croatia, where she still lives with her husband, their son (read boss!) and the son's pet rabbit named Shhh! (or some other gibberish that's the favorite of their son for the day.)

She spends her days driving her husband up the wall (when he can't get her ass up from the bed in the mornings), reading and daydreaming, or following orders from a three-year old. In the hectic life she leads (and loves every second of it), she never thought about writing. But, then one day a name popped in her head, then, the snippets of things, and she sat down and started typing. Next thing, she wrote a book. And now, she's trying to write another one 😊 ;)

Also, by Ana Balen

Good Intentions Volume One
https://www.amazon.com/gp/product/B07QK3Z73R/

Good Intentions Volume Two
https://www.amazon.com/gp/product/B07ZQKLRMV/

Good Intentions Volume Three
https://www.amazon.com/gp/product/B083VW1Q64/

Good Intentions Trilogy Box Set
https://www.amazon.com/gp/product/B084V8R6GH/

Wishing For A Star
https://www.amazon.com/gp/product/B07DGM7TQ5/

Never Too Late (part of Christmas Wishes box set)
https://www.amazon.com/gp/product/B07XXJPMW9/

www.ingramcontent.com/pod-product-compliance
Lightning Source LLC
Chambersburg PA
CBHW031333160726
47993CB00002B/646